W9-COT-835

WITHDRAWN

St. Louis Community College

Library

5801 Wilson Avenue
St. Louis, Missouri 63110

WORKING ROBOTS

In this picture, a big T^3 industrial robot is welding an automobile body.
Cincinnati Milacron Inc.

WORKING ROBOTS

Fred D'Ignazio

ELSEVIER/NELSON BOOKS
New York

Library of Congress Cataloging in Publication Data

D'Ignazio, Fred.
Working robots.
Bibliography: p.
Includes index.
Summary: Presents an overview of the various kinds of working robots, or intelligent
machines, and their growing impact on the economy and society.
1. Robots, Industrial. [1. Robots] I. Title.
TS191.D53 1982   629.8'92   81–17279
ISBN 0–525–66740–7   AACR2

Published in the United States by E. P. Dutton, Inc., 2 Park Avenue, New York, N.Y.
10016. Published simultaneously in Canada by Clarke, Irwin & Company Limited,
Toronto and Vancouver.
Editor: Virginia Buckley   Designer: Trish Parcell
Printed in the U.S.A.   First edition
10 9 8 7 6 5 4 3 2 1

for
Troy, Eric, Laurel, Abby,
Catie, Shannon, and Michael—

I hope that working robots become your
servants, your assistants,
and maybe even your friends.

CONTENTS

Photographs appear after pages
30, 62, and 78

ACKNOWLEDGMENTS

A great many people contributed to this book. You all know who you are, and I am very grateful for your help.

I feel some people made special contributions to this book, and I would like to give special thanks to them here.

Virginia Buckley   You are a super editor. Thanks for being so patient. Thank you especially for your perceptive guidance and your expert suggestions and editing.

Janet Letts D'Ignazio   Thanks for taking care of Catie, Eric, the telephone, the taxes, and the bill collector while I finished this book.

Libby and Babe D'Ignazio   Thanks for being my cheerleaders and bankers.

Abby Gelles (Robotics Institute)   Special thanks to you, Abby. You were by far my most generous, my most valuable source of information on robotics.

Mike Glick, Larry Miller, John Baicy, Parker Silzer, and *Duffy Gilligan* (Universal Printing)   A long-overdue thanks for your extraordinary "Kodaking" under fire.

Jim Gupton (author-inventor)   Thanks for all your books, photographs, time, and attention. You made a significant contribution to this book.

Dana M. Sally and Faye J. Martin (Alfred T. Brauer Library) Thanks to the two most outstanding, patient, and helpful librarians I have ever known.

I would also like to thank Jim Albus (National Bureau of Standards), Marty Auman (National Bureau of Standards), Peter Blake (Robotics International of SME), Ken Davis (General Development), the editors at *Robotics Age,* George Gregoire (Microbot), John Johnston (Hydro Products), Jonathan and Flora Kaplan, Erik Lindholm (Lour Control), Jock McClees (Terrapin), Bob McGhee (Ohio State University), Lori Mei (Robot Institute of America), Ellen Mohr and Lynne Novicky (Unimation), Hans Moravec (Robotics Institute), D. J. Reynolds (inventor), Carl Ruoff (Jet Propulsion Laboratory), Harley Shaiken (MIT), and Barry Spaeth (Cincinnati Milacron).

INTRODUCTION

Robots in the form of mechanical humans, animals, aliens, or monsters are part of our movies, our culture, our myths, and our legends. But until the dawn of the computer age in the late 1940's, independent, "thinking" robots were not possible. Even the most complex, lifelike machines were mere electrically or mechanically powered automata devices that repeated the same functions over and over, with little or no interaction with the outside world, except to be switched on or off.

With the invention of the first electronic computers, four major breakthroughs in robotics, the science of robots, occurred.

First, a single computer—or a computerized robot—could now be infinitely reprogrammed: After a robot had finished performing a task, its electronic memory could be wiped clean and a new list of instructions loaded in. With different programs, a robot could perform an unlimited number of different tasks, or the same task over and over again.

Second, scientists began finding ways to make computers

smaller and smaller. In the late 1940's, scientists invented the solid-state *transistor*. This little device eventually replaced all the big, hot vacuum tubes that used to act as a computer's logic and memory circuits. Later, in the 1950's, scientists found ways to take these transistors and other circuit elements, shrink them to microscopic size, and then combine them into a single *integrated circuit* (IC). ICs became so small that, in 1968, a scientist built an entire computer on a cornflake-sized square of silicon called a *chip*. Since then, scientists have devised ways to squeeze bigger computer memories and ever more powerful computers onto smaller and smaller chips. "Computers on a chip" have made real robots possible, since the robot's computer brain can now fit inside the robot's body. And that robot brain is more powerful than room-sized computers of only twenty years ago.

A third boost that computers have given robots are the new, tiny *microelectronics* circuits now being built that give a robot "eyes" and "ears," a voice, and a sense of touch. These devices are called *sensors*. They are electronic versions of human senses that enable the robot to capture, store, and analyze information from the outside world, then use that information to help guide its future actions.

Fourth, ever since computers were first invented, people have been using them to *simulate,* or mimic, the processes of the human brain—processes such as thinking, understanding, and learning. Scientists who study the brain and find ways for the computer to imitate it have started a whole new field, called artificial intelligence (AI).

Where will we first see real working robots? The first working robots are already among us, working alongside human beings in our factories. In fact, industrial robots are already so popular—and so profitable—that they are supporting some of the technologies that gave them their start. Robots will also soon appear in our homes and in our classrooms.

Tiny, cheap ICs have made it possible to manufacture desk-top computers that are less expensive than an average color TV. These typewriter-sized machines are not only good for balancing checkbooks, playing games, or drilling facts and figures into students' heads. Hobbyists are taking these small computers and *hooking them up to robots.*

For the first time in human history, people are building real working robots. Teachers and students are building robots in the classroom. Hobbyists are building them in their basements. Scientists are building them in their labs, manufacturers in their factories.

Large companies and government and university researchers are designing factories and offices of the future in which robots will do all the work under the control of a super-robot "foreman." Scientists are designing seeing, walking robots that can explore other planets, perform undersea mining, or service an oil pipeline. And hobbyists are building robots that can talk, respond to voice commands, play games, operate free of human control, learn, and even evolve a lifelike personality.

These are the "working robots" that you will meet in this book, robots destined to play a growing part in your life: robots that are real—not those from movies or science fiction.

This book is not a "how-to" book, it is an idea book. It does not tell you how to build a robot. It is the book you read *before* you read the how-to books and try to build a robot on your own. It will tell you what working robots are, how they are put together, how you can "teach" them, and what they can do. It is an overview of all the various kinds of working robots.

This book will also show you the growing impact of robots on our economy and our society. More robots are definitely coming, and with them will come serious problems as well as enormous benefits.

Perhaps most important, you can use this book to get ready

for robots. It can help you decide what part you want robots to play in your life, whether to see them as a social problem, an economic boon, an interesting hobby, a course at school, a lifelong career, or all of these things together.

WORKING ROBOTS

1

WHAT IS A WORKING ROBOT?

Let's say you are in a department store, and you see a crowd of people gathered around a mechanical man holding a vacuum cleaner in one hand and a stack of dishes in the other. The mechanical man vacuums the floor, then rolls over to a table and sets down the stack of dishes. Meanwhile it is carrying on a conversation with members of the crowd. It is even whistling while it works.

At first you think the mechanical man is operating entirely on its own. Then you notice two men at the edge of the crowd. One man is speaking into something concealed in his hand, presumably a microphone. This man is the source of the mechanical man's "voice." The other man has his arm in a large paper sack. He is operating the mechanical man by remote radio control. The question is: Is this remote-controlled, housekeeping mechanical man a real working robot? Your answer might well be yes.

In our modern, highly mechanized society we see all sorts of ingenious, human-created devices that seem to be robots. They beep, talk, buzz, blink lights, walk or roll around, delight, frighten, and entertain us. But are all these machines really robots? Just what constitutes a real working robot?

Or let's say you are leaving a parking lot. You stop at an automatic gate. The gate swings up. It was set into motion by the car's tires when they passed over a pressure-sensitive rubber strip. The gate responded entirely on its own. No human was nearby to lift it or flick a switch. The question is: Is the gate a working robot arm?

Your immediate answer is probably, "No, the gate is not a robot." But why not? What makes the mechanical man a robot, and the automatic parking-lot gate not a robot? What are the basic necessary characteristics of any robot? Does it have to look like a person or an animal? Does it have to talk, growl, or sing? Must it have moving parts? Must it be mobile? Does it have to be made of metal?

According to a new set of standards now being adopted by robot hobbyists, scientists, manufacturers, and users, neither of these machines is a real working robot. Instead, some machines (like the housekeeping robot) are what are known as *teleoperators,* devices remotely controlled by human beings; others (like a steam shovel) are *human amplifiers,* devices that increase human strength or agility; and still others are *automata,* machines (like your turntable) that may automatically perform a number of tasks but cannot be reprogrammed and do not respond to external *feedback*—information from the environment—once they are turned on.

Examine your own images of robots and try to figure out what makes one machine a robot but not another. Why are many people's images of robots so deep-seated? If robots were a new phenomenon, this would not be the case, but robots and robotlike creatures go back to the farthest reaches of human history. We have been fascinated with real and imaginary imitations of ourselves at least as far back as the paintings on cave walls created by our remote ancestors.

Like Narcissus, the character in the Greek myth who loved to look at his reflection in the water, we take pleasure in looking at reflections of ourselves, and the more lifelike the reflection, the more pleasure we experience. In fact, human history can even be seen as our attempt, using the art, science, and technology at our disposal, to make the imitation humans (the robots) of each era more sophisticated, more refined, and more lifelike than ever before.

From the late Hellenistic period on—about two thousand years ago—humans have been busy building mechanical automata to delight, entertain, and sometimes serve other humans. As far back as 200 B.C., Heron of Alexandria is said to have created automated theaters complete with exploding flames, dancers, and whirling gods. Through the Dark Ages, the Middle Ages, and the Renaissance, the Arabs and later the Europeans kept this tradition alive, coming up with increasingly sophisticated mechanical creations, including talking heads and fortune-telling "computers."

Evil, menacing automata also appear frequently throughout history, from the story of the Jewish Golem that walked through sixteenth-century Prague to Mary Shelley's Frankenstein. Present-day plays, movies, and science-fiction and fantasy literature include villainous creatures such as HAL, the computer in Arthur C. Clarke and Stanley Kubrick's *2001*, and the homicidal robot Maximilian in Walt Disney's *Black Hole*.

Interwoven with the traditions of the good and bad automata are the equally important traditions of real versus fantasy automata. On one hand we have the rich mythology, folktales, and literature based on automata that are clearly imaginary; on the other we see the development of real machines. But the two tracks are not always separate. On numerous occasions automata have surfaced that gave the illusion of being something they were not. One of the most famous fraudulent automata was Von Kempelen's chess-playing machine, which defeated chess masters all over Europe, scoring its most famous victory over Napoleon. On the surface it appeared to be controlled by an intelligent "computer." In fact, it was controlled (according to some accounts) by a legless Pole who was a political refugee from Russia and was making a living playing chess from inside the machine's cabinet.

This brings us back to what constitutes a robot and what does not. One standard might be that *a robot must be a real machine capable of actually doing what it appears to be doing.* This eliminates all of the fraudulent machines as well as the entertainment robots of movies and TV, which appear to be independent, thinking creatures but are typically costumes worn by men or women, elaborate models, or, occasionally, remote-controlled devices.

However, two even more important standards have been developed. The first is that true robots are computer-controlled. This helps us eliminate a number of "near-robots," such as *prosthetic* devices (artificial limbs); *exoskeletons* (metal frames surrounding human limbs to give a person "bionic" power); *telecherics* or *teleoperators* (remote "manipulator" arms); and *locomotive devices* (walking vehicles occupied by a human operator). These near-robots fail to qualify as true working robots because they do not have the ability to operate on their own. Here is the first standard:

> A real working robot must be autonomous and independent, at least partly free of external control from a human operator. It must be a general-purpose device that, on different occasions, can perform different functions. To do all these things requires that a robot be under the control of a programmable computer.

But it is not enough that a robot is under computer control. It must also have sensors, sensing devices that mimic organic senses, such as vision, hearing and the sense of touch. It should be capable of responding to external stimuli as well as to programmed internal commands. So here is the second standard:

> A real working robot must interact with its environment and have at least a limited sense of self-awareness. It must be able to receive information from its environment, act on this information in some manner (e.g., grab an object with its manipulator, or arm), and receive new information, or feedback, describing the result of that action.

In a nutshell, then: *A real working robot must be under computer control, and it must have senses.*

These two standards are new, and they are tough. Not everyone agrees with them. But they are rapidly gaining acceptance among the three groups of people most involved in the field of robotics: (1) the robot hobbyists and experimenters; (2) the university scientists and researchers; and (3) the manufacturers, distributors, and users of commercial (largely industrial) robots.

On the other hand, these standards do not include most of the ten thousand robotic arms that are working in factories all around the world, since these arms, though under computer control, are not equipped with sensors. But this situation is only temporary. A new breed of working robots is being planned that will be under microcomputer control and also will contain sensors to enable the robots to "see," "hear," and "feel." This is also true of hobbyist robots.

I like the new standards. I think that the microcomputers and the new machine sensors being developed make it certain that these standards will soon be universally accepted. On the other hand, I'm going to make a few allowances in this book for near-robots that are not quite up to these standards, such as devices built by hobbyists that are not true robots. These machines are a good illustration to beginners on how they, too, might get started building their own robots.

Occasionally I will focus on robot "toys" that are of special merit. Though not true robots, they can be easily modified to become real robots. And since they are relatively inexpensive, they represent a good way for low-budget, beginning robot builders to get their feet wet.

I will also mention and include pictures of teleoperators, or remote-controlled vehicles. These machines, which are partly or entirely under the control of a human being rather than a computer, may have limited sensory capabilities. I mention them because they are nevertheless very complex devices; because they perform a useful function that eventually might be performed by a true working robot; and lastly, because more and more, with the addition of onboard computers and sensors, these devices are evolving into real working robots.

All these standards, which appear so tough and so rigid now, will eventually become as obsolete as the other robot standards that preceded them. Robotics and artificial-intelligence technology are advancing very rapidly. Robots that will be produced ten or twenty years from now will bear only a remote resemblance to the most advanced machines we are capable of producing today.

Still, we have a long way to go before we can even begin to approach the level of robotics or artificial intelligence embodied in the robots we read about in science fiction or see on TV or in the movies. Thus, with robot technology sprinting forward, it would be foolish for us to come up with rigid standards we will only have to discard later. We need to come up with flexible, practical standards of what constitutes a robot, standards that reflect the current state of technology as we see it. In this light, there are *no* robots in existence today. Instead, what we have are all sorts of devices in transition, machines that are on their way to becoming real robots.

Until recently, most robots were handmade or at least built with machine tools operated by humans. But at an advanced robot-manufacturing plant in Greenwood, South Carolina, half of all machines used to build the robots are numerically controlled (NC) machines, primitive robots in that they can perform a sequence of operations—like welding or lifting —while under the control of a numerical program. NC machines are not as flexible as true robots: They are not computer-controlled or easily programmed, and they lack the vision and tactile sensors common on advanced robots. Nevertheless, they operate at two or three times the speed of humans, and they can work day after day, three shifts (24 hours) at a time, without breaking down.

The speed of industrial robots and their relative low cost and reliability are causing many companies to reshape their whole manufacturing process so that they can include robots in key locations. The same is true for the robot manufacturers themselves. New robot-building plants now on the drawing boards will use the companies' own robots to build new ones. Perhaps the most advanced robot-building plants are located in Japan. In one plant, robots work around the clock to make three new robots a day, a hundred new robots a month.

The next step is the fully automated robot-building factory. In these factories of the future, robot teams will operate under the careful eye of a computer "foreman," who, in turn, will report to a plant-supervisor computer. New robots will be designed on computer terminals. A limited number of humans will work among the robots, installing them, training them, repairing and maintaining them.

2

TYPES AND PARTS
OF ROBOTS

Before we try to understand what robots are made of, it's a good idea to learn more about the major categories of real working robots. Some of the major categories, along with some of the robots' major parts, are described here.

INDUSTRIAL ROBOTS

All have armlike projections and *grippers* (hands or pincers); they are computer-controlled and operate on their own, once programmed. They include *pick-and-place* robots, which move objects from one place to another; *programmable* robots, which can be led through their steps or programmed with a "teach box"; *computerized* robots, which have an onboard minicomputer or microcomputer and use a flexible programming language; *sensory* robots, *welding* robots, and *assembly* robots. In the past, almost all industrial robots were large, heavy machines. Many newer industrial robots are small and light and can pick up and manipulate only light items. These

8

small, new industrial robots are the precursors to the clerical robots and "gopher" robots that will eventually appear in offices, retail businesses, and industries like banking and insurance.

LABORATORY ROBOTS

These include advanced industrial robots with sophisticated microcomputer brains, new multi-jointed arms, or advanced vision or tactile senses. Some laboratory robots are being developed that have remarkable hand-eye coordination; others are mobile; still others have legs and walk.

EXPLORER ROBOTS

The only true explorer robots that are already in operation are the outer-space probes developed by NASA. These machines, which have sophisticated sensory systems, are advanced remote-controlled vehicles, but they can also be computer-controlled.

However, a whole new generation of computer-controlled, sensor-equipped explorer robots is under development in laboratories around the world. These robots include mine-exploring mice; seeing, walking undersea robots; rolling plane-tary explorer robots; and walking Earth-based robots. And some of the remote-controlled vehicles that already exist are evolving into true explorer robots.

HOBBYIST ROBOTS

Hobbyist robots come in all shapes and sizes. Most hobbyist robots in the past were not true robots, but newer hobbyist robots are being built with microcomputer brains and various vision, tactile, speech-synthesis, and speech-recognition systems. Most hobbyist robots are mobile and run on wheels.

Many have arms and grippers. Some are controlled over a cable (or by radio control) by a home computer. Most hobbyist robots are either "robot pets" or "robot assistants." There are few (if any) true working, housekeeper hobby robots, the ultimate goal of many hobbyists.

CLASSROOM ROBOTS

Most classroom robots today are hobbyist robots. Real classroom robots will come into use after the general acceptance of classroom computers and will be used to teach basic skills to young children, such as hand-eye coordination and simple math and logic skills. But this is just the beginning. Classroom robots will also be used to teach advanced math, physics, art, and design. A classroom robot might someday appear in the form of a mobile computer that rolls around the room and acts as an "intelligent assistant" to a busy teacher.

ENTERTAINMENT ROBOTS

A new generation of real entertainment robots is arriving. These robots operate under microcomputer control and often appear at promotional events, on TV and radio. The entertainer robots may talk to people and respond to spoken commands.

ROBOT POWER

Two of the most important parts of robots' bodies are the robot power source and the robot arm. A robot must have power if it is to move. Power can drive a robot's wheels, its legs, its arms, its shoulders, hands, and wrists. Most types of robot grippers (hands or pincers) need their own power to pick objects up, hold them, and release them.

The power for a robot comes from its drive system. There

are four major types of robot drives: *electrical, mechanical, hydraulic,* and *pneumatic.*

Electrical and mechanical systems work together and are known as *electromechanical systems.* These systems are frequently used by hobbyist robots, especially to drive the robots' wheels. Electricity is sent along a wire from a battery or wall outlet to the robot. It can power all sorts of electrical motors —*servomotors, stepping motors, pulse motors, linear solenoids,* or *rotational solenoids.* The electric current sets up a magnetic field in the motor, which drives the gears, thus converting electrical energy to mechanical (or physical) energy. Depending on the type of gears used (worm, spur, bevel, et cetera) and the level of voltage generated, the electric motor will operate the robot's wheels at a given speed and a given *torque* (a turning, twisting force). The amount of torque the motor generates will affect how fast the robot moves going uphill, downhill, or carrying a particular load.

If there is an electric motor for each of the robot's two wheels, and the motors work *bidirectionally* (in both directions), the way to make the robot turn is to have the motors turn in opposite directions. For example, to make a robot turn right, you program its computer to move the right wheel backward and the left wheel forward. If a robot is built with four wheels, the front two wheels usually are separately powered by electric motors, and the rear two wheels may be simply two free-rolling casters—plastic or metal wheels such as those on the legs of a bed.

Electric power is used by small hobbyist robots and by smaller industrial robots. But many industrial robots (about 30 percent) use a *pneumatic* (air-pressure) system to operate, which is cheaper and more reliable than other methods. Pneumatic drives pump air into small cylinders. The large amount of air forced into a small place quickly builds up enough pressure to power part of a robot, often the smaller parts, such as its grippers.

Hydraulic power is the most popular method used on industrial robots. Although *hydraulic* means "moved with water," hydraulic drives on robots pump a thin kind of oil, not water. Hydraulic drives are like pneumatic drives except that they are usually larger and pump oil, instead of air, into a cylinder. When the cylinder is filled with oil, a piston drives forward and forces a particular part of a robot's body to move. Usually this is a big, heavy part of its body, such as a shoulder or a telescoping arm. Hydraulic motors and cylinders are compact, generating high levels of force and power, and they enable a robot to make very accurate, exact movements.

THE ROBOT ARM

A robot's *manipulator* is really a combination shoulder, arm, wrist, and hand. All these together enable a robot to reach for an object, pick it up, carry it, and put it down. A robot's *sphere of influence* (or work area) is the sum of all the locations in space where the robot's hand can get to some object, either to manipulate it or to perform some operation, such as welding or painting.

For an arm to move its wrist and hand to any place in its sphere of influence, it needs a minimum of three *articulations*, each with its own drive system. These three articulations—or paths of motion—are: (1) *extend* and *retract* arm (out and in); (2) *swing* or *rotate* arm (left and right); and (3) *elevate* (lift) arm and *depress* (lower) arm. There are three types of motion for a robot's wrist: *bend* (roll forward and backward), *yaw* (spin from right to left or left to right), and *swivel* or *roll* (roll down to the right or left).

Thus if an arm has three paths of motion, and the wrist has three, the robot can pick up and manipulate any tool or object its gripper can reach. In robot jargon, this robot has a full *six degrees of freedom,* meaning that the robot can move its arm and wrist in any of six independent directions. Compared to a human, however, this is still limited motion. Your shoulder, arm, and hand combined have a total of forty-two degrees of freedom.

Robot arms are an exciting part of any hobby robot because they enable the robot to interact with—and change—its environment. The arm can be programmed to specialize in any number of tasks. For example, you could teach it to manipulate chess or checker pieces, or you could program your robot to use its arm to plug itself into a battery recharger whenever its battery got low. Before building a robot, you should consider all of the types of hands a robot might have. Humans, of course, have only one type of hand, but robots can come with a variety, including mechanical (handlike) grippers, hooks, spatulas, scoops, ladles, electromagnets, vacuum suction cups, and sticky fingers (with an adhesive).

Figure out what you want your hand—and arm—to do. Since human homes and human tools are all designed to be operated by general-purpose human hands, it might be wise for you to make your robot's hands a lot like your own—capable of gripping, pushing, pulling, grasping, and releasing.

PROSTHESES: ARTIFICIAL LIMBS

If you are interested in building a robot and you want it to have arms, hands, and maybe even legs, you should learn as much as you can about *prostheses* (artificial limbs). You might consider buying a prosthesis to put on your robot.

There are two basic kinds of prostheses: powered and unpowered. Powered prostheses use tiny rechargeable batteries or compressed gas. The latest prosthetic arms use hydraulic power coming from a portable power unit or from batteries for energy storage. The new prostheses are made of light materials such as plastic, thin wire cables, and microelectronic circuits, including microcomputers.

3

THE ROBOT BRAIN

The brain is perhaps the single most important and exciting part of a robot's body. It can be constructed from mechanical parts such as gears and pulleys, or by using different electrical circuits and components such as transistors, diodes, and resistors. But these methods have become obsolete for serious robot builders since the invention of the *microcomputer* and the single integrated circuit. Scientists have developed methods that enable them to fit more and more components onto smaller and smaller integrated circuits. Colin Norman, in his report *Microelectronics at Work* (Worldwatch, 1980), writes,

> By 1980, the most densely packed circuits contained close to 100,000 components on a silicon chip measuring just five millimeters across, and the aluminum conductors linking them together were about 30 times thinner than a human hair. In three decades, a roomful of vacuum tubes, wires, and other components has been reduced to the size of a cornflake.

By 1990, experts believe we may be constructing cornflake-size integrated circuits with 10 million to 100 million different components. A single chip will be more powerful than today's largest computers. This reduction in size has also made it possible to produce computers at a fraction of their former cost.

Since electronic circuits have decreased in size and price so dramatically, is it now possible to build a robot version of a human brain and have the robot brain imitate the human brain's functions?

Someone once said that to build a working model of the human brain you would have to construct a building the size of the Empire State Building and fill it with electronic circuits. Then, to get it to work, you would have to plug it into the hydroelectric generators at Niagara Falls. But thanks to the extraordinary miniaturization of electronic circuits, in only a few more years, a computer with the same number of circuits as the human brain will be small enough to fit inside the robot brain and be powered by a 9-volt transistor-radio battery.

Does this mean that, in only a short time, we might construct robot brains as powerful as human brains? Yes and no. The basic problem is that we still have only the faintest notion of how the brain works. Thus, no matter how tiny we make the electronic components for a robot brain, we have no idea how to combine those components into an artificial, or imitation, human brain.

Robot brains (and computer brains in general) are extremely fast. A single operation in a human brain might take several milliseconds (thousandths of a second), but that same operation in a high-speed robot brain might take only a few *nanoseconds* (billionths of a second). That makes robot brains a million times faster than human brains.

For some tasks, such as performing lightning-fast arithmetic or retrieving information from memory quickly, the robot brain is clearly superior to the human brain, due to its higher speed. On the other hand, if we ask a robot (with vision, tactile, and acoustical sensors) to "pick up the green triangular block underneath the black cubical block behind the dining-room chair," then we had better be prepared to wait a long time and hope that the robot can figure everything out.

The point is that the human brain, though slower than a robot brain, processes many types of information *at the same time*. The best way to look at a human brain is not as a collection of tiny wires, but as an enormous collection of billions of interacting tiny computer brains. This makes it easy for even a three-year-old human, for example, to obey the "fetch the block" command while the robot is still scanning the room trying to figure out what a chair looks like.

THE INSIDE OF A ROBOT'S BRAIN

A robot's computer brain has three major functions: *storage* (memory); *processing* (decision making, arithmetic, logic); and *input-output* (receiving and transmitting information).

All of the robot brain's functions occur in the form of extremely rapid pulses of electricity, signifying to some part of the brain the presence, or absence, of an electrical charge. If a charge is present (or high), it is represented by a one ("1") *bit* (binary digit). If it is absent (or low), it is represented by a zero ("0").

All information stored and processed by the robot brain is represented as sequences of ones and zeros. Grouped together eight at a time, these ones and zeros are called *bytes*.

Using a special code, each byte can represent a letter, a number, or a symbol. Several bytes together can store a large number used in an arithmetic calculation or a word or one of several dozen commands to the computer.

A typical robot brain (on a hobbyist robot) is built by taking several computer chips and plugging them into a plastic *printed-circuit* (PC) board. Usually there will be a *central processing unit* (CPU) chip to handle logic, arithmetic, and decision-making functions. This chip is also referred to as the *microprocessor.*

There will be one or more *Random Access Memory* (RAM) chips to store information and commands while the robot's power is turned on. There will be several *interface* chips that enable you to plug the robot brain into other devices, such as a keyboard, a small picture screen, or sensors, such as speech-recognition circuits or a video camera. Finally, there will probably also be one or more *Read-Only Memory* (ROM) chips, which have a *control program* permanently stored in them. The control program oversees, schedules, and coordinates all the computer chips on the circuit board. It makes it easier to operate the robot's brain and feed it instructions.

ROBOT BRAINS AND HUMAN BRAINS

So what can we do with all of this raw computer brain power? Although the new microprocessors cannot successfully imitate all the complexities of the human brain, they will allow us to construct robot brains that are simplified models of it. The human brain is organized hierarchically from simple "computers" at the bottom to complex "computers" coordinating things at the top. We can imitate it and construct robots that have simple microprocessor chips to control the arms, the hands, the wheels, the videocamera eyes, and so on, and we can use microprocessor chips with complex programs to coordinate all these simple microprocessors.

The simple microprocessors will be concerned simultaneously with very detailed stimuli, including the reflection of light from several objects in a room, the measurement of the distance from the robot to those objects, the weight of the object in the robot's hand, and the voltages rippling through the robot's microphone "ears."

The "high-level" microprocessors, on the other hand, will be concerned about the robot's goals, its currently assigned tasks, the status of those tasks, and its physical sensations—its summary "impressions"—of the outside world.

This is the same way your brain works. The human brain has a small processor—a *neuron*—devoted to monitoring and controlling every fiber of every muscle in the human body. For example, ten times every second, inside the retina of each of your eyes, ten million tiny neurons are reacting to a flood of light entering the pupil of the eye. Ten times every second, these ten million cells "burp" up a gigantic byte of information and shoot it to your brain along the optic nerve.

Do you "see" these hundred million bytes of visual information every second—just from a single eye? The answer is no. Your brain's lower-level neurons—its *subprocessors*—take care of things. They organize and summarize this flood of visual information and send it to your high-level neurons —your "conscious" mind—as a single sensation that tells you just two things: an object's brightness and its color.

The goal of robot builders is to build robot brains that do the same thing—but on a simpler level.

CURRENT ROBOT-BRAIN PROJECTS

We soon might see robots that use dozens, even hundreds, of microprocessors in the same way the human brain uses its tiny computers composed of neurons.

Already, the new, more powerful processors are appearing on robots. For example, Reggie, a robot designed by Ken Davis of Phoenix, Arizona, uses three separate microprocessors.

Hans Moravec, a research scientist at the Robotics Institute at Carnegie-Mellon University in Pittsburgh, Pennsylvania, is experimenting with a mobile robot "cart" that employs sixteen processors, which are organized hierarchically like those in the brain. Certain processors are specialists devoted to tasks such as the robot's vision or controlling its motors. Meanwhile, one processor acts as the "controller" for all other processors.

Scientists are also working to develop *ultracomputers,* machines composed of a complex network of perhaps thousands of tiny microprocessors. The work is only at a theoretical stage, but if the scientists are successful in developing an ultracomputer, we may have taken our first small step toward creating a robot brain that is capable of duplicating the functions of the human brain.

In terms of robots, this work is critical. We already have computers that can perform logical and mathematical computations far faster than human beings can. But we still do not have robots that even come near a seven-year-old human in coping with a complex, swiftly changing outside world. One method of narrowing this gap is by using new artificial-intelligence programs. Another method, perhaps just as promising, is to develop a new generation of computers composed of thousands of parallel, simultaneously interacting, microprocessors.

4

HOW TO TEACH
A ROBOT

How does a robot know what to do? The answer is: You have to teach it. How you teach it depends on the type of robot it is. You can "teach" one type by operating a control panel at its base. To teach many factory robots, you use a *teaching pendant* or *teach box* (a metal box with buttons and knobs). Another method is to lead the robot by the hand or arm. Many experts believe that the most popular method of teaching robots in the future will be to give the robot a *program*—a sequence of commands stored in a robot's memory. Received one at a time, such commands are obeyed by the robot's brain. Today, people have to type programs into the robot's memory using a *keypad* or typewriterlike *keyboard*. In the future, people may be able to give a robot its orders—its program—simply by talking to it.

TEACHING A ROBOT TO PICK AND PLACE

There are three major types of robots being used in factories. First, there is the *limited-sequence* robot, which uses a combination of mechanical "stops" and limit switches to control its hand and arm. When the switches turn the robot's drive on, the robot arm moves. When the robot arm gets to where it's going, the drive is switched off. The arm bangs into a metal stop that is cushioned with a shock absorber to protect both itself and the arm. Then the drive is switched on and the robot's arm is moved to the next position. Because of the nature of its movement, this type of robot is sometimes called a "bang-bang" machine. The robot's program is in the form of a group of control wires attached to a plugboard. To change the robot's actions, you have to rewire the plugboard.

The *point-to-point* robot is another major type of industrial robot. It is like the limited sequence robot in that you can only tell the robot arm to "begin at point *A*" and "finish at point *B*," but you cannot tell the robot the path to follow between point *A* and point *B*. A teaching pendant is used to program this kind of robot.

A third type of industrial robot is the *continuous-path* robot. An example of this robot is Unimation's new Apprentice. This $35,000 robot is small as industrial robots go, weighing only 125 pounds. But it can perform a number of tasks, including arc welding, where it holds a welding gun and moves it along a complicated seam to weld two metal parts together. It could be used to weld heavy farm equipment, automobile parts, construction equipment, ships, and steel building structures.

Unlike the earlier robots, the Apprentice can follow an exact, continuous path to an accuracy of 0.04 millimeters (less than one five-hundredth of an inch). To teach the Apprentice, the human trainer takes the robot hand and leads it along the path it is to follow. As the Apprentice's hand is moving along the path, its brain is quickly taking samples of each position the hand passes through. The brain sends sixty of these "position" samples to memory every second. Later, when the robot is ready to begin its job, it can play back each of these positions and move its hand accordingly.

When the human trainer is leading the robot hand, he doesn't have to move the hand at its final operating speed. If he is moving it over a jagged, complicated seam, he can go slowly. Later, the robot can be speeded up so it does the welding much faster. Yet even at the higher speed, doing the task over and over again, the robot is still amazingly accurate and never deviates from the exact path it was trained to follow.

LANGUAGES FOR INDUSTRIAL ROBOTS

Although most factory robots are taught with teaching pendants and by leading their arms or hands, newer robots are appearing that obey commands the human trainer enters on a keyboard located near or on the robot's body. The commands are all part of a special language that the robot understands. A command can be stored in the robot's brain as part of a program to be run later, or it can be routed directly to the robot's brain (its microprocessor or CPU) to be decoded into electrical pulses and obeyed immediately.

Each robot language comes with a special translator program (called a *compiler, assembler,* or *interpreter),* which takes the command the human trainer types in and translates it into the sequence of binary (high/low or on/off) electrical pulses that the robot's brain can understand. For example, the translator might take a command such as "SWIVEL ARM 45 DEGREES" and convert it into machine language. What would look to us like a long string of ones and zeros (say, "100111000011000011100 00001111111110101010100"), would actually be a high-speed sequence of pauses and +5 volt electrical pulses sent to the robot's brain.

There are two types of industrial-robot programming languages: the low-level *explicit languages* that tell the robot what to do in great detail, such as "RAISE JOINT #4 NINE MILLIMETERS AT AN AVERAGE VELOCITY OF 20 MM/SECOND," and the high-level *implicit languages,* such as "LOAD PALLET" or

"WELD FIXTURE." Before the high-level commands can be sent to the robot's arm and hand, the robot's brain has to translate them—first into low-level commands, then into the bits, or electrical pulses, that the hand and arm can obey.

A person can program a robot much more easily and quickly using a high-level language, since a single high-level command might translate into dozens of low-level, or explicit, commands. Also, by making it simple to program the robot, it is possible for a factory worker who is an expert at a particular job to program the robot, instead of having a robot expert or computer programmer do it. In this way, the robot can learn a new job faster, cheaper, and probably better.

What are some standard industrial robot languages? Just as with human languages, there are a lot of them. Among the explicit languages, you'll find VAL, EMILY, SIGLA, and WAVE. Among the implicit ones, you'll see AL, ROBOT APT, AUTOPASS, RAPT, and MAL. Also, among the implicit languages, standard nonrobot computer languages have started to appear, such as FORTRAN and PASCAL.

But all these languages are only intermediate and temporary ways for humans to train and communicate with working robots. Factories will soon become more fully automated and computer-controlled. Eventually, there will be layers upon layers of computers operating robots, and computers supervising other computers. We're going to have to develop more advanced, more standardized languages to operate these factories of the future, which will be completely automated—from the time the raw materials enter the factory to the boxed and labeled manufactured product that goes out the door.

A single human being sitting in a command center should be able to look into a computer picture screen and instantly see which robots are working, what they are doing, which robots are broken, what the inventory of materials is, how many products have been produced that day, and so on. The person should be able to intervene quickly and easily at any step in the manufacturing process to solve a problem or take care of an emergency. To do this will require a powerful, easy-to-use language; clear, colorful graphics screen displays; and a *data base* that stores the information on every person, tool, computer, robot, and machine part or piece of equipment involved in the manufacturing process.

LANGUAGES FOR LABORATORY ROBOTS

There are three basic types of laboratory-robot languages used by scientists and engineers: (1) machine languages in the form of ones and zeros or low-level commands of an explicit language; (2) high-level, artificial-intelligence languages; and (3) very high-level, *natural* languages that resemble spoken human languages such as English.

Machine languages don't look much like English. But their low-level, assembler-language commands do enable people to control precisely everything the robot does.

LISP, a type of high-level language, is also used with laboratory robots, especially when scientists wish to write programs that cause the robot to exhibit some artificial intelligence. A robot demonstrates artificial intelligence when it mimics some feature of human intelligence, such as learning or self-awareness. LISP is an unusual-looking language, most notably in its extensive use of parentheses—and parentheses inside of parentheses. Like the "programming" that controls the human brain, LISP is good at manipulating *symbols*—of ideas, concepts, or physical objects like "dog" or "flower."

LISP programs can be organized hierachically, just as the human brain is organized. This lets you easily build a program to imitate functions you normally see in the human brain. For example, you can create a LISP program whose lower levels act as *subprocessors,* doing all the detailed work (much like the neurons in the lower "primitive" levels in the human brain);

and whose higher levels receive reports from the lower levels and engage in higher-level tasks such as synthesizing information and making decisions (in much the same way as the cortex does in the human brain).

Also, LISP is an "interactive language" (known as an *interpreter*). You can use a keyboard and type commands into your LISP robot's memory and watch the robot's brain evaluate them as soon as you enter them. If the robot does something unexpected, you have a *bug,* or error, in one or more commands. You can try to *debug* the commands. As you type the new commands in, the robot will obey them and you will see if your bug is gone.

Late in 1969, scientists at SRI International in Menlo Park, California, completed the first version of a mobile, computerized robot named Shakey. Although not even nearly ready to cope with life outside his tiny microworld room, Shakey, even by today's standards, was a pretty smart robot. Shakey's brain was an elaborate program called STRIPS ("Stanford Research Institute Problem Solver, which STRIPS away subgoals as it goes"). Like the human brain, it was organized hierarchically, with lower levels feeding information to higher levels, and higher levels instructing the lower levels to carry out their decisions.

Scientists could give Shakey English-like commands via a radio link from another computer. Once he was up and running, Shakey was entirely self-programming, and when the scientists wanted him to do something, they just told him in very general, humanlike terms.

Shakey had mapped out his microworld, so scientists could tell him to "GO TO POSITION (x,y)," and Shakey would do it. Or scientists would say simply, "PUSH THE THREE BOXES TOGETHER." Shakey would buzz around the room, use his TV camera "eye" to find three boxes, and push them together. This is pretty remarkable, since Shakey had to know what a "box" is and then recognize three of them. He had to understand what "push" means, he had to know what "together" means —especially when one is talking about boxes.

Another command scientists would sometimes give Shakey was "PUSH THE BOX OFF THE PLATFORM." Since Shakey had no arm, he had no way to reach out and push the box off the platform. What could he do?

Actually, Shakey was such a bright robot, he figured out —without being told by the scientists—that in order to reach a box, he would have to climb up the platform. In order to climb the platform, he would have to find and climb up a ramp. He rolled around the edge of the platform and found the ramp. He rolled up the ramp, found the box, and pushed the box off the platform.

Shakey was one of the brightest robots of his day, yet he was still only on a par with a two-year-old. Today, according to scientists, we have some robots capable of obeying instructions that would challenge a five-year-old. The robots have a long way to go, but they're catching up.

A LANGUAGE FOR THE ROBOT TURTLE

People have been building mechanical animals for thousands of years. However, these creatures were only automata. They lacked a programmable computer brain, and they had no sensors to supply them with information from the outside world. Instead, their mechanical gears, springs, belts, and pulleys, or their electrical switches and relays caused them to perform "mindlessly" the same sequence of movements over and over again, until they were shut off.

Beginning in the 1920's and 1930's, new automata of all sorts became very popular. These devices still had many mechanical parts, but they were electrically powered and often had one or more electrical sensors.

Harry Piraux's Philidog was typical of the new group of

electromechanical animal automata. Philidog had photoelectric sensors, which enabled him to spot and approach a light
source, such as a flashlight. When he got close to the light,
Philidog began to bark. He would continue barking until the
light was removed.

Sparko, an automaton dog, was even more sophisticated
than Philidog. Sparko became quite a celebrity when he was
exhibited along with Elektro, his android "master," at the New
York World's Fair in 1939. Sparko had heat sensors as well as
light sensors. When fairgoers walked by, Sparko would be
attracted to the heat in their legs and would chase after them.

A turtle robot invented by Grey Walter in Great Britain in
the 1950's is another example of an ingenious automaton, a
near-robot. Walter's turtles had three wheels. They had two
photoelectric cells for eyes and a microphone for ears. Their
turtle shell was connected to *strain gauges,* so that any pressure
put on the shell would cause a signal to be sent to the turtles'
electrical brain. The robots' power came from a rechargeable
battery.

Using a complicated circuit diagram, Walter wired the turtles
to do a number of tricks. They could "freeze" or go forward
when Walter whistled at them. They would approach light
sources, and they could negotiate their way around obstacles
placed in their path.

Walter's turtles attracted a tremendous amount of interest
(and affection). They also spawned several "generations" of
electrical and mechanical imitations. Late in the 1960's, turtle
inventors decided to hook up a computer to their turtles and
thereby turn them into true robots.

The Terrapin Turtle, designed by Dan Hillis at MIT's
Artificial Intelligence Lab, is one of the latest offspring of
robot turtles. It has no onboard power supply, so it needs to be
hooked up to an external source of power such as a battery.
Also, the Turtle has no computer "controller" onboard. To
give the Turtle a brain, you need to connect it to a home or

classroom computer via an "umbilical-cord" cable. The cable is plugged into two of the computer's *parallel ports*, "doors" that allow several bits of data to enter or leave the computer at the same time.

Inside the outer insulating layer of the cable are twelve wires. Four of these wires carry signals from the Turtle to the computer. They are like a four-lane, one-way highway for data coming into the computer through its "input" port, enabling the Turtle to send four bits (binary digits—ones or zeros) to the computer.

The other eight wires carry signals from the computer back to the Turtle. The "output" parallel port is like a doorway out of the computer, and the eight wires are like an eight-lane, one-way highway from the computer to the Turtle. They enable the computer to send eight bits at a time to the robot.

All the "on" (or "1") bits must be transmitted at a level of at least 2 volts. This is known as a *high TTL level*. All the "off" (or "0") signals are transmitted at a level of from 0 volts to no more than 0.6 volts. This is known as a *low TTL level*.

What information does the robot send the computer? The Turtle has four touch sensors mounted right under its Plexiglas dome. If the robot encounters an obstacle, the dome is pushed down, and one or possibly two sensors are depressed. The computer controller can read the four-bit signal coming from the Turtle and tell if any of the sensors are depressed. If no sensor is depressed, all four sensor bits (the four incoming bits on the input "highway") are ones, but when a sensor is depressed, it will send a zero along the cable to the computer.

If the computer wants to give orders to the Turtle, it uses the eight "output" wires connecting it with the Turtle.

If the computer wants the Turtle to do something, it sends a high-TTL voltage (a "1" bit) along the particular lane that controls one of the Turtle's "organs"—its beeper (high and low tones); its writing pen ("up" if not writing, or "down" if writing); its two blinking *light-emitting diode* (LED) eyes, and its two wheels, each controlled by a separate motor.

You would get pretty tired if you always had to program the computer to operate the Turtle by using long strings of ones and zeros. Fortunately, there is an easy solution to this problem: You can program the computer in a high-level language called BASIC. Your program can have several special sets of instructions called *subroutines,* which translate from BASIC back to the string of ones and zeros to be sent to the robot, and from the ones and zeros sent by the robot back into an English message or a BASIC command.

To make your program even easier to operate, you can create a set of Englishlike commands to operate the Turtle, such as PENUP, PENDOWN, FORWARD 10 (inches, centimeters, turtle-lengths, et cetera) or RIGHT 90 (degrees—a right turn). To do so, you will have to write a program that recognizes the command when it is typed in on the computer keyboard. Then the program will GOSUB (jump) to the appropriate subroutine and order the Turtle to do whatever you want.

Turtles are becoming very popular as classroom robots. Two good ways to put them to use is to write Turtle geometry and artificial-intelligence programs for them. To write the Turtle geometry programs, you must figure out ways to get the Turtle to draw different geometric shapes—squares, circles, rectangles, triangles, hexagons, spirograms, helices, spirals, cubes, and so on. As you practice with the Turtle and watch it obey your commands, you'll get ideas for increasingly complex and more beautiful shapes.

To write an artificial-intelligence program to get the Turtle to explore and find its way through mazes, you'll need to set up some subroutines that tell the computer when a particular Turtle touch sensor is depressed. Then you'll have to build into the program a response for the Turtle, depending on which sensor or sensors are depressed. This way, every time it bumps into a wall in your maze, the Turtle will turn or back off and try a new direction. As the Turtle explores the maze, you might gradually enable it to build a "map" of the maze in its (the computer's) memory. The memory would also be storing important information, such as which passages were dead ends and which had been explored. Meanwhile, the Turtle can show you where it has already been by keeping its pen down so that it will leave "Turtle tracks" through the maze.

This thimble is full of tiny, solid-state *temperature sensors*. Installed on a robot's body and wired to the robot's miniature computer brain, these sensors could give the robot a sense of "hot" and "cold." *Motorola Inc.*

The Turtle robot is computer-controlled—over a long wire "leash." It knows when it bumps into something, thanks to its pressure sensors, located beneath its Plexiglas shell. *Terrapin, Inc.*

Herman, a remote-controlled "mobile manipulator," sees through two TV camera "eyes." He works as a troubleshooter in dangerous, high-radiation areas, such as inside a nuclear reactor.

Oak Ridge National Laboratory and Union Carbide Corporation

Cincinnati Milacron T^3 robots are built at a new, spacious robot-manufacturing plant in Greenwood, South Carolina. Here, human "inspectors" are checking three robots for the last time before shipping them out of the plant.   *Cincinnati Milacron Inc.*

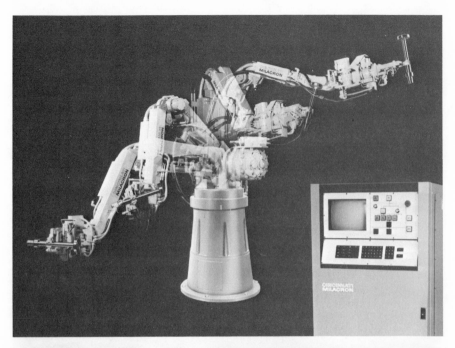

This Cincinnati Milacron T^3 robot is really a giant arm that can reach and grab objects from floor level to a height of 12 feet.
Cincinnati Milacron Inc.

A human factory worker is using tweezers to pick up tiny computer "brain" chips and place them, one at a time, in a protective package.
Texas Instruments Inc.

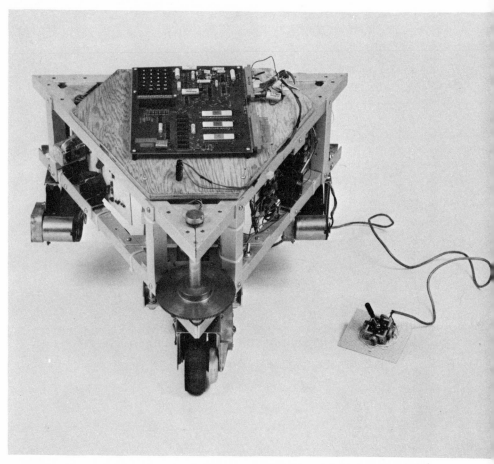

An early version of Tod Loofbourrow's robot Mike. Mounted on top of Mike is a circuit board with several computer chips that make up Mike's "KIM-1" microcomputer brain. *Photo reprinted with permission from Hayden Book Company, Inc., and The Art Works Photography. Photo originally appeared in Tod Loofbourrow,* How to Build a Computer-Controlled Robot *(Hayden, 1978).*

A human worker can train a factory robot by programming it using a teaching pendant—a control box attached to the robot's computer by a wire cable.
Cincinnati Milacron Inc.

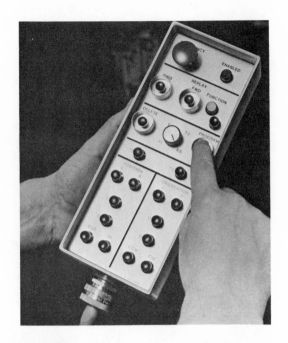

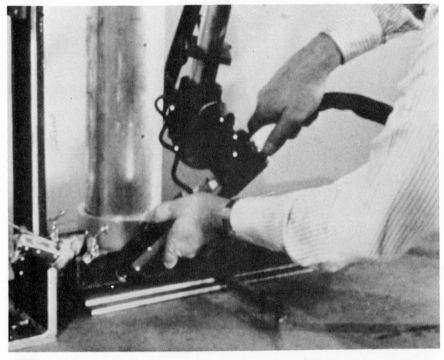

A human trainer is teaching Unimation's Apprentice robot by guiding its arm along the path it will later follow when welding two pieces of metal together.   *Unimation Inc.*

By installing the SpeechLab circuit board on your robot, you can get it to obey up to sixty different, single-word, spoken commands. To help the robot understand you, you must speak loudly, clearly, and use a microphone.

Heuristics, Inc.

SPEAKER

DISPLAY

POWER SUPPLY

CONTROLLER

SYNTHESIZER

WORD STORAGE ROM

SOLID STATE SPEECH™ MODULE

This is the inside of Texas Instruments' popular *Speak & Spell.* The "Synthesizer" is a tiny computer chip that generates a humanlike voice. Its vocabulary is stored on "Word Storage ROM" chips. The computer's program can be changed by plugging in a "Speech Module"—a computer memory chip with the new program stored in the memory.

Texas Instruments Inc.

This is a close-up of the Omneye CCD (Charge-Coupled Device) vision chip. The chip—shown alongside the tip of a person's finger—is actually a high-speed, solid-state TV camera that can be used as a robot's eyes.

Hughes Aircraft Company

This robot has a camera mounted on its wrist, which it uses to locate and assemble machine parts.

National Bureau of Standards

5

ROBOTS AND
THE OUTSIDE WORLD

As we have seen, a true working robot must be controlled by a programmable computer, it must be able to acquire information about the outside world, and finally, based on its computer program, it must make decisions and take actions based on that information.

We have spent the last two chapters looking at a robot's computer brain and learning how to program that brain. Now we are going to take a look at ways in which robots can acquire information about the outside world—with "senses" such as speech recognition, speech understanding, machine vision, and a sense of touch. We are also going to examine newer ways for robots to interact with the outside world—using robot speech, robot music, robotic hand-eye coordination, and robot movement—on wheels and on legs.

SPEECH RECOGNITION

Computers play a major role in the next few sections because the computer is the part of the robot that controls its senses and interprets the information they collect.

A robot's computer is accustomed to getting information in a very artificial manner. First, you have to type in the information or commands to the computer. The computer scans what you have typed in, looking for *word boundaries*. These boundaries make it simple for the computer to break apart, or *parse,* your message into separate words that it can decode and then obey.

The robot's computer can also be pretty picky. Unless you are careful and adhere to the rules of a particular computer language, the computer may reject what you have typed and flash something like a "?" or "WHAT?" on the screen to show you its confusion.

Now consider human speech as a means of sending information to a robot's computer. When you give a verbal command to the computer, that command does not always sound the same. For example, "PRINT A+B"—when written—always looks the same to the computer. But when the command is spoken, it's a different matter entirely. The command can be spoken loudly or softly, rapidly or slowly. The speaker might be a man, a woman, an old person, or a child. He or she might use a crisp staccato voice or a slurring drawl, or the voice might have a strong ethnic or regional flavor. It might even reflect that the speaker is happy, sad, angry, lonely, or just plain tired.

There are other complications as well. For example, the room where the speaker is giving the command may have good acoustical (sound-carrying) properties or it may badly distort the command. The speaker might be talking into a microphone or shouting from the other side of the room. All these variations make computer speech recognition terribly difficult.

Many robot builders use sound to communicate with their robots. But they have to be careful. For example, Jonathan Kaplan's Electronic Workman robot responds to his voice, but only when he says a single letter of the alphabet at a particular *pitch* (a particular sound frequency, or note).

Other roboticists have used whistles to control their mechanical pets. Generally, whistles are easier for a robot to understand than a voice because they produce a pure pitch with only slight variations each time the robot's master whistles.

Tod Loofbourrow, one young roboticist, built a voice-recognition unit on his robot Mike. Mike can obey a set of eight verbal commands, such as FORWARD, STOP, RIGHT, and LEFT. To begin with, Tod speaks the eight commands into Mike's microphone. Each command is separately stored in a command table called a *buffer*. When Tod gives Mike a verbal command, Mike analyzes the sound wave created by Tod's voice. If a close match is found between the current command and the "master" command, Mike recognizes and obeys it. He immediately moves forward, backward, turns, or whatever.

However, if a close match is not found, Mike rejects the command and continues wandering around Tod's living room. Tod sees that Mike hasn't recognized the command, and he can either let Mike ignore him, or he can say the command again, this time being careful to speak very clearly.

Tod's voice-recognition system for Mike works surprisingly well most of the time, and yet it was relatively simple to install and cost Tod only ten dollars in parts.

Mike's system is an example of a *speaker-dependent, discrete word recognizer.* It is "speaker dependent" because Mike's master command table only has Tod's voice stored in it. Each person has his or her own unique *voiceprint,* or sound wave.

Mike can recognize eight of Tod's sound waves—eight of Tod's verbal commands—but not anyone else's.

Mike's system is a "discrete" word recognizer because he can recognize only one word at a time. He cannot, for example, recognize a *command string* of two or more commands spoken one immediately after the other.

What sort of robot speech capability should you look for in the future? Before too long, robots will be equipped with *continuous-speech, speaker-independent, speech understanding* systems. This means the robot will recognize several spoken words at a time—maybe even complete sentences. The robot will also recognize the commands even if they are spoken by different members of your family or class. Eventually the robot will not only recognize what you are saying, it will *understand* what you are saying. This means the robot will relate each of your spoken words to a whole range of ideas, concepts, pictures, associations, and so on. It will try to place what you are saying into a larger context.

There are already in existence numerous computers that can perform automatic speech understanding. Unfortunately, they are not small, general-purpose microprocessors, but full-size, special-purpose computers costing as much as $70,000. And though they may recognize continuous speech, they can be ridiculously slow in trying to understand it. For example, in some laboratory systems, it takes a computer an hour and forty minutes to understand something that it took a person only thirty seconds to say.

You can already install a speech-recognition system on your robot so it can recognize simple one-word spoken commands. But you'll probably have to wait some time before you can buy or build a system that will let every member of your family have long, meaningful, human-to-robot discussions.

SPEECH SYNTHESIS

Our speech-synthesis technology is farther along than our technology for speech recognition or speech understanding. There are four primary techniques you might use to get your robot to talk back to you. First, you can use a method like Tod's, where your robot *digitizes* your voice. This method is called *pulse-code modulation.* Second, you can buy a speech chip and some ROM chips with someone else's voice already digitized. Third, you can buy a speech chip that generates a number of canned words completely from scratch. Or, fourth, you can "build" words from speech sounds, such as *phonemes* and *allophones.*

If you use the first method, it means you need to equip your robot with a microphone that enables it to translate—or *transduce*—your voice's sound wave into electrical pulses. Then the robot takes samples of these pulses and codes them into the binary bits—the ones and zeros—it can store in its memory and understand.

Later, when the robot's program calls for it to say something, the robot recalls the digitized words as a string of ones and zeros. It shoots these bits through a *digital-to-analog converter,* which translates the on-off pulses of electricity to a continuous wave of *voltage* (electrical pressure) levels analogous to the final sound wave.

The robot sends this electrical wave through a filter to catch any *noise* (high- and low-frequency pulses); then through an amplifier to boost the pulses; and, finally, to a speaker. The voltages force the speaker's cones to vibrate and generate waves of sound rippling through the air.

A large voltage causes the cones to vibrate rapidly. A swiftly vibrating cone sends a large number of sound waves skipping through the air. We hear this high-frequency burst of waves as a high pitch, or treble note.

A small voltage, on the other hand, causes the speaker cones to vibrate slowly. The slowly vibrating cones send fewer sound waves into the air. We hear this low-frequency group of waves as a low pitch, or bass note.

A person's voice is a combination of these low notes and high notes. If the low notes predominate, the person's voice sounds deep. If the high notes predominate, the person has a high voice.

The voice coming from a robot sounds much like the voice of the human who programmed it. How close the match is depends on the quality of the equipment used, especially the microphone, the filter, the amplifier, and the speakers.

Perhaps the most important feature, though, is how fast your robot takes samples of the voice, and how many samples it can fit into its memory. The general rule is: the more samples, the better. But this takes a fast computer and a lot of RAM memory, two things most robots still lack.

If you are thinking about building a talking robot, you are doing your thinking at the right time. Computer-synthesized voices are fast becoming a booming business. Talking chips with anonymous electronic voices are finding their way into digital watches and clock radios, TVs, toy dolls, video games, microwave ovens, washing machines, typewriters, and automobiles. They come with several "canned" messages. The microwave will tell the cook, "Your roast is done"; the car will nag the driver with "Please fasten seat belts"; and the typewriter will scold its owner when he misspells a word.

A major concern, in fact, is that so many of our appliances will soon be talking to and about us that they will create a new form of noise pollution. On the other hand, these voice chips will be a godsend for blind people and for those who are verbally impaired.

The Votrax SC-01 is a good example of a new speech synthesizer that may soon be used by robot builders and by visually and verbally impaired people. The SC-01 is small and inexpensive, and with it, you can build a large vocabulary for your robot. It will translate any word in that vocabulary into understandable speech using an expanded group of sixty-four synthetic phonemes (word sounds).

If you buy the chips by themselves, you can mount them on a circuit board, add a filter, an amplifier, and a small battery power supply, and then plug them into your robot. Your robot's program will control the chips directly. This way, whenever your robot wants to tell you something, it will just go ahead and say it.

If you are the do-it-yourself type, you can install both speech recognition *and* speech synthesis on your robot probably for less than $200. Important features to watch for when shopping for your robot's voice are how big the speech-synthesizer's vocabulary is, how many samples per second were taken to digitize the voice, and, most important, how it sounds.

One inexpensive way to obtain a complete synthesizer chip, filter, and amplifier is to buy a talking toy. If you are handy, you can take the talking equipment out of the toy and install it directly into your robot.

THE MUSICAL ROBOT

If you are going to build a robot that talks, why not have it play music as well? A number of companies now make music-synthesizer boards for small computers. (See "Materials and Schools" for their names and addresses.)

Your robot can play up to sixteen notes simultaneously, and in stereo. Also, you can enter music in sheet-music format and create sound waves that come remarkably close to those produced by several different musical instruments.

ROBOT VISION

Look around. What do you see? Do you see your school library? The living room? Your bedroom? Your mom?

Now look again. Don't you also see patterns of color? Of light and dark? Of edges and intersecting lines? Don't you see everything in a three-dimensional perspective, with larger, near objects hiding some of the smaller, more distant objects?

Look a third time. Aren't many of the objects you see clearly in motion, some entering the "scene" and some disappearing, even as you watch? Can you now see a great number of details in the scene, details that you could focus on and name, but usually don't? For example, you might see bark and branches and roots and leaves but lump them into something you know as a "tree"; and you may lump dozens of trees together into "woods" or "forest." As you look, try to pick out things that are strange, unfamiliar, or that you can't name. It's pretty hard, right? You know the names of just about everything you see.

Now think what this familiar scene must look like to a newborn baby. *Or a newborn robot.* Neither has acquired names for any of the objects in the scene. Neither has any real idea of perspective, of three dimensions, of one object sitting in front of another without swallowing it up. Neither understands what motion is, where things come from when they enter the scene, or where they go when they leave.

Vision is not something that just happens the moment you first open your eyes. Vision is a learned behavior. It depends entirely on your brain's interpretation of the complicated shapes, shades, and hues that flow like a flood through the retinas of your eyes. This flood of visual data is disjointed, and meaningless by itself. To give it meaning, you must connect the pieces into patterns. And the only way you can form patterns is with knowledge, ideas, experiences, memories, and associations. These supply you with *templates,* master images to compare with the scene you are now viewing. Slowly, as your library of master images grows, you begin to fit together the pieces of what you see. After a while, these pieces begin to come together naturally. You find yourself combining smaller images into larger images, until finally everything you see has some overall meaning.

Humans acquire vision through a growth, learning and development process that begins sometime before birth and continues for years afterward. Robots are acquiring vision, too, not as developing individuals, but collectively, as successive "generations" of an evolving "species." Hobbyist robots and early industrial robots are acquiring the rudiments of vision—the building blocks, such as the perception of light, darkness, color, and motion; and the detection of edges, surface textures, and contours.

There are two major reasons why providing vision for robots is a major task. First, a single scene contains an enormous amount of information. For example, a typical black-and-white TV set picture is composed of about 8 million bits of information—just to make a single clear picture. And these pictures are sprayed onto the TV screen at thirty times a second! Even the larger minicomputers are incapable of handling this much information.

Second, even if the machines' memories could store all this information and process it, we still don't have the *algorithms* (the procedures, or programs) to analyze it in any reasonable amount of time.

There are two ways of adding vision to present-day robots. One way is to limit a robot's vision to simple obstacle detection. Robots have a hard time recognizing—and a harder time *understanding*—what they see, but it is relatively easy to get a robot to "see" that some object, such as a chair, is blocking its path.

Hobbyists are building robots with infrared sensors, photoelectric sensors, ultrasonic sensors, and laser range finders. Tiny robot mice use as many as four infrared sensors to see the cardboard walls of mazes. Robot turtles, equipped with photoelectric cells, are attracted like moths to candles and flashlights. Robot pets imitate bats (and Polaroid cameras) by bouncing high-frequency sound waves off furniture and people around them. The distance of the object from the robot can be determined precisely by the amount of time it takes the sound wave to boomerang back to the robot.

One hobbyist, taking lessons from cats, is building robots with *optowhiskers*. The whiskers are really an "extended-range infrared proximity sensor" that can detect a human hand up to three feet away and a piece of white paper up to four feet. The infrared whiskers are an inexpensive way to give vision to your own robot.

Industrial robots, laboratory robots, and advanced hobbyist robots are gradually evolving more complicated *optical* vision systems (systems based on light). Still, even with these systems, the robot's recognition task should be limited to a small number of objects in a carefully controlled environment.

How does a robot's optical vision work? We can get a simplified picture of this process by taking a look at a vision system developed by General Motors for use on its assembly-line robots. First, a *vidicon* (video camera) or a solid-state *Charge-Coupled Device* (CCD) camera is mounted either on the robot itself or next to the robot. For example, the camera captures pictures of machine parts lying on a temporarily idle conveyor belt. Each picture is composed of hundreds of horizontal lines that show the varying gray levels (brightness levels) of an object. These gray levels can be digitized (converted into binary codes) and stored in the solid-state camera or in the robot computer's memory. Later, they can be converted back into brightness levels to produce a picture on a TV screen.

By itself, however, this picture is useless. As far as the robot is concerned, it just has a string of bits, or a long list of brightness codes, stored in its memory. Several tricks and techniques are required before the robot can "make sense" of the picture it has stored. For example, the robot may use *edge-detection* techniques to try to locate the major edges of the objects in the picture. This enables the robot to build the edges into objects, such as machine tools.

Many robots' vision systems stop at this point. A "pick-and-place" robot doesn't need to interpret *what* it sees, it only needs to distinguish objects from shadows and from the background (such as the conveyor belt). Then, once it has the object's range (distance) it can extend its arm, pick the object up in its gripper, and carry it to the next location in the manufacturing process.

More sophisticated robots, such as robots designed to package and assemble parts, must be able to recognize several different objects. One of the major methods used to help a robot recognize an object is called *template matching*. It works in the same way Tod's robot, Mike, recognizes Tod's spoken commands. The robot compares its image of an item sitting in front of it on the conveyor belt with a group of master images, or templates, stored in its memory.

But what if the object on the conveyor belt—say, a connecting rod, a bracket, or a gear—is turned upside down and backward from the image—the template—stored in the robot's memory? How is the robot going to make a match? A human would be able to match the two objects instantly, but to a robot, they seem to be entirely different.

At this point, some robots take either the template or the image of the current object, and—on a special TV picture screen or in the form of mathematical equations—they begin rotating it and *scaling* (shrinking or enlarging) it. This helps the robot compare the template to the object from several different angles. Eventually, the template and the rotated, scaled object will look similar, and a match will have been made. But this process is complex, and on a fast-paced conveyor line the robot's computer recognizes objects too slowly to keep up with the line.

Fortunately, researchers have come up with an alternative. They ask the question: Even if the object is in a different position from the template, what is there about the object that makes it similar to the template, no matter what its position? This might be the same question our own brain asks when we see an object and attempt to recognize it.

There are, for example, an object's *concurves*—its "connected curves," or straight lines and circular arcs. Most objects will come to rest in a few stable positions after being placed on a conveyor line. When seen in each of these positions, the object will *always* have the same number of straight lines and curves.

When a robot sets about detecting the edges of an object, it can make note of these concurves, measure them, and count them. Then it can compare this information with similar information on its templates. This is a relatively simple and quite fast process, and it enables the robot to locate quickly the correct template or at least the best two or three choices for a match.

New military, industrial, and commercial robots with vision systems are demonstrating that, in many situations, it can be quite profitable—in terms of increased accuracy or productivity—for robots to see. Hence there is a big push to develop robot vision systems.

SRI International has developed a vision module that will help robots determine the identity, position, and orientation of parts on the assembly line, thus enabling them to perform material-handling, inspection, and assembly tasks. SRI's vision module employs a solid-state camera, and it can be programmed by using the Robot Programming Language (RPL). A robot equipped with the module can scan boxes moving down a conveyor line. Even though the boxes are randomly positioned on the line, the robot can find the upper right-hand corner of each box, attach a stencil, spray the stencil with ink (thus labeling the box), then remove the stencil—all while the boxes are moving.

A vision module is also being developed and tested at the National Bureau of Standards. The system is remarkable because it lets the robot recognize an object by its three-dimensional shape. The vision module also uses a *stroboscopic* (flashing) light source to help the camera obtain an ideal image of the item. The robot's camera is mounted on the robot's wrist, so it can easily be positioned to take pictures of an object from many different angles, which greatly helps the robot to recognize an object.

As with human eyes, the robot's vision system itself does not recognize the object. It just gathers the relevant visual information—the picture. The line, angle, and curve data from the vision system are used by the robot's high-level computer to identify the part. Similarly, the human brain uses the eyes and subprocessing neurons (nerve cells) to gather visual information, then it manipulates this information in the high-level *visual cortex* in order to recognize a particular scene.

OTHER SENSES FOR ROBOTS

We have talked about robot speech recognition, robot speech synthesis, robots that play music, and robots that see. Are these all the senses, or capabilities, that we can give our robots?

Think about your own body. What other senses do *you* have?

Try an experiment. Close your eyes. Now stretch one of your arms into the air in any direction. Reach as far as you can. Now stretch out your other arm and, with your eyes still closed tight, try to bring your second hand around to touch your first hand. Now open up your first hand, and, with your second outstretched hand, try to touch each of your fingers.

The question is: How do you know where your hands are? You don't see either hand. You can't hear your hands. You don't smell them or taste them. How do you know how to bring them together?

The answer is you use *kinesthesis*, the sense that tells you where your arms, legs, feet, and hands are. It does this by measuring the angle of your joints, the weight on your muscles, and how much your muscles are extended or stretched.

Now, one more quick experiment: Close your eyes and bend your head any way you want. Now, using the index finger of your right hand (or your left), try to find your nose and tap it lightly. Next, find your ear. Find your eyebrow. Find your tongue.

This ability to "know" where your head is comes in part from your kinesthetic sense. It comes also from the *vestibular organs* located in your inner ear. These organs give you your sense of balance—the ability that keeps you from toppling over when you stand up, run, ride a bike, or climb a mountain.

A final sense that you have that is important to mention is your sense of touch, *somatothesis*. Touch, in fact, is only one of your body's "skin senses." Others include the sense of pain, of hot and cold, and the sense of pressure on the skin.

When scientists and hobbyists build robots they try to include machine versions of all these senses on the robots. (The reason we didn't review the sense of taste or smell is because few, if any, people are building robots that can taste or smell things.)

Many robot inventors, especially in industry, feel that it is more important to give a robot a sense of touch than vision. They point to the number of tasks a blind human can do, just using the sense of touch.

There are various devices that you can use to give your robot the sense of touch. Many are *pressure transducers.* They translate pressure (pushing or weight) into an electrical signal. The more you push, the bigger the signal.

Pressure transducers are often referred to as "touch sensors" or "impact sensors." A popular impact sensor is the *ribbon switch,* a long strip of wire that converts sudden pressure into electricity. Tod Loofbourrow, for example, installed ribbon switches all around the base of his robot Mike. Every time Mike makes contact with an object, the ribbon switches generate a pulse of electricity to Mike's brain. Tod has Mike programmed to recognize when he has bumped into something and to back off quickly.

Microswitches and *strain gauges* are two other types of touch sensors. A microswitch is a tiny switch that can be installed on the robot's body or arm. It is tripped when the robot bumps into something or grips an object.

Strain gauges and other devices, such as *torsion springs, tension switches,* and *tension springs,* are often used in robot hands. When the hand grips something, the springs act as an electronic scale and measure the weight of the object. Then they adjust the amount of power the arm and hand will need to pick up the object. These sensors can also adjust a hand's gripping force, enabling it to become so sensitive that it can pick up an egg without breaking it.

The technology of robot arms and hands is moving forward rapidly. Scientists and students at MIT have built a robot arm with fourteen joints, three elbows, and hydraulic "muscles." The arm is operated by its own arm computer.

In Japan, scientists have invented a powerful, flexible hydraulically powered hand that can do many things the human hand can do. The three fingers of the hand are like a human's thumb, index finger, and middle finger. The fingers, with a total of twelve joints, can do many complex tasks, such as tie a knot or fasten buttons. And, of course, they can use chopsticks.

Micropressure transducers have been invented that can be built into a robot's arm and hand. These tiny circuits will enable the robot to imitate your skin's ability to feel pressure. A sensor developed at MIT, for example, can sense pressure at 250 points in a single square inch, and it can "feel" something as light as a person's finger.

BUILDING A MOBILE ROBOT

Deaf, dumb, and blind robots do best if they don't move at all. That's why most robots used in industry are stationary devices, often bolted to the floor. In the past, it was a challenge to the robot's simple brain just to operate a single arm to do its work.

Since microcomputers that control robots are now powerful and cheap, why not use one to control a robot's arm? Then, if that works, why not give the robot several arms—like an octopus? Every thousandth of a second all the arm computers could report to a central head computer. The robot's head computer could coordinate all these arms to keep them working together and prevent them from bumping into each other.

Scientists are also working with seeing robots to help them develop better *hand-eye coordination,* gradually teaching their robots to use their arms and hands in more efficient ways, based on what they see.

Furthermore, scientists are now building smart, sensing robots that move. Some of these prototype moving, seeing robots are humorous looking. The mobile robot at the Jet Propulsion Laboratory at Caltech, in Pasadena, California, for example, looks like a big farmer's wagon with a railroad-crossing gate and a pygmy stoplight on the front, and a hefty filing cabinet on the back.

In fact, the "gate" is a sophisticated robot arm, the "cabinet" is a powerful minicomputer, and the "stoplight" is the robot's TV camera eye. The onboard computer and the solid-state eye enable the robot to solve the two main problems of robot mobility: guidance and path selection. Simpler robots in the past used what was called the "dead-reckoning method" to move. They would look around, decide on a destination, plot a path to that destination, then take off. If the robot bumped into an obstacle on its way, it would stop, look for its destination, and head off again.

To keep from stumbling over moving obstacles in their path,

people—and the new seeing robots—use a guidance system. As we move we look all around and constantly update our picture of the path to our destination. If, all of a sudden, something steps into the path, our processor goes into "emergency" mode and we try to stop, step back, or dodge the unexpected obstacle. Eventually we reach our destination, usually without having bumped into anything on the way.

The newer laboratory mobile robots use an advanced guidance system. Their eyes may not always recognize what it is they see in front of them, but they can quickly spot a nearby obstacle—even a mobile one, such as a person—and their computer can take rapid evasive action.

Another robot that appears humorous until you get a closer look is the Cart, invented by Hans Moravec of the Robotics Institute at Carnegie-Mellon University. According to the inventor's own description, the Cart looks just like a card table on bicycle wheels, only taller. On the front of the Cart is something that looks like a blackened mixer-blender; on a high perch on the back sits something resembling a tall bird feeder. Mounted on what looks like a bookcase on the center of the Cart is what appears to be a small telescope.

Again, appearances can be deceiving. The "bird feeder" is really a radio antenna for sending and receiving radio signals; the "telescope" is an advanced TV camera that is controlled by nine separate microcomputer brains. The Cart, which has received national publicity, has been described as a "nine-eyed robot." Its nine eyes come from the robot's camera, which runs up and down a track and shoots pictures from nine horizontal locations.

The Cart moves slowly: Every ten or fifteen minutes, it makes up its mind where to go and lurches forward. According to Moravec:

> After rolling a meter, it stops, takes some pictures, and thinks about them for a long time. Then it plans a new path, executes a little of it, and pauses again.

It works slowly, because computers are at their worst in trying to do the things most natural to humans, like seeing and common-sense reasoning.

The Cart performs flawlessly indoors. But the course it follows is so complex that, as slow as the Cart is, it still has to swerve three or four times to avoid hidden obstacles it cannot see until it is practically on top of them. Even so, the Cart can maneuver itself through the 20-meter indoor course without bumping into a single obstacle.

The Cart does very well with only its video camera eyes. However, if a robot can have nine eyes, why not give it nineteen or ninety? HILARE, a French robot, is different from the Cart in that it is equipped with other forms of vision sensors in addition to its TV camera. These sensors include a laser range finder, a triangular radar system (with two infrared emitter-receivers), and numerous ultrasonic sensors placed all around the robot's three-wheeled, triangle-shaped, cartlike body.

Moravec's "mild-mannered machine" and HILARE with its numerous "bat" eyes are only tentative first steps toward robots that can roll out the front door into the big wide world outside. Yet scientists are already looking forward to the day when descendants of the Cart can prowl around other planets, exploring and performing scientific experiments; and descendants of HILARE can roam around giant automated warehouses, finding, hauling, stacking, and shipping materials.

Boris Dobrotin of the Jet Propulsion Laboratory at Caltech in Pasadena, California, sees a time when mobile, seeing robots will assemble automated space stations and work in space factories. On Earth, meanwhile, he sees a "fully automated urban traffic system" in which robot Carts of the future, carrying people and cargo, dodge back and forth through obstacle paths of congested traffic and crowded intersections.

WALKING, CLIMBING ROBOTS

Are all mobile robots in the future going to roll around on wheels? Or will some of them resemble the gigantic Imperial Walkers in one of the *Star Wars* episodes, and amble across rough terrain on mechanical legs?

There is a growing number of applications for nimble, agile robots equipped with legs and feet. One application already being seriously considered is maintenance of the Alaskan oil pipeline across the thousands of miles of tundra in Canada and the United States. According to environmental experts, a wheeled vehicle would damage the fragile ground and disturb the ecology of the area. Light, legged robot mechanics, however, could be employed to walk along the pipeline. They could monitor and inspect it and quickly radio emergencies such as oil leaks, malfunctioning equipment, or acts of vandalism or sabotage.

Legged robots might also be used undersea, in mining operations on Earth, and in the exploration, mining, and industrial operations on the moon and on other planets.

Walking *drone* operators with human operators inside, such as the numerous walking carts that have been invented for use by handicapped people in place of wheelchairs, have been around for years. But these "robots" are really *human amplifiers* rather than true working robots. They lack both computer control and sensory feedback from the environment. Moreover, it is difficult for human operators to control all the joints of a walking robot.

Walking, computer-controlled robots are a recent invention, but already there are many of them taking their first steps in laboratories in the United States, Japan, and the Soviet Union. The Soviet Union, for example, has a walking *hexapod*—a six-legged robot that can travel over almost any terrain at the relatively rapid speed of 6 kilometers per hour. Its six legs are arranged into two stable tripods, and it walks by moving one tripod forward while the other one acts as support. The legs are jointed, so the robot can raise and lower itself. It uses a scanning laser range finder to survey the surrounding terrain up to a distance of about 10 to 15 meters.

In the United States, Ohio State University scientists have built a six-legged, computer-controlled robot they call the OSU Hexapod Vehicle. Like the Soviet hexapod, the robot is being tested on irregular, "off-road" terrain. As the robot walks, its computers constantly adjust the legs to the terrain in order to equalize the weight on each leg, prevent foot slippage, and prevent the robot's motors from being overloaded.

In the future, advanced versions of this robot may be used in hazardous situations such as fire fighting, underground mining, the disposal of bombs and other explosive or toxic substances, and to carry radioactive materials in and out of nuclear reactors.

ROBOTS IN INDUSTRY

If every instrument could accomplish its own work, obeying or anticipating the will of others . . . If the shuttle could weave, and the pick touch the lyre, without a hand to guide them, chief workmen would not need servants, nor masters slaves.

—ARISTOTLE, *Politics*

Aristotle wrote these words over two thousand years ago. What he envisioned—shuttles that could weave, lyres that played music—were intelligent, self-controlled machines, what we now call "robots." He also anticipated the logical application of these machines as automated servants—replacements for human workers and laborers.

People struggled for over two thousand years to build Aristotle's smart, self-motivated machines. But the world's technology was too primitive. Now, thanks to inventions such as the computer, television, and the laser, we are on the threshold of creating the marvelous "instruments"—the automated servants—that Aristotle foresaw.

51

But if these working machines are truly robots, shouldn't they resemble human beings? According to *Webster's Third New International Dictionary,* a robot is a "machine in the form of a human being that performs the mechanical functions of a human being but lacks emotions and sensitivity." Many books, movies, and plays have been written about "worker" robots, all of whom were in the form of human beings.

But why must robots be machines created "in the image of man?" Aristotle did not envision his automatic lyre and shuttle in human form. And the thousands of robots working in factories today do not even remotely resemble human beings.

Many observers visiting factories are shocked when they first see the robots. They enter expecting to see Hollywood, or science-fiction-type robots—classical "mechanical men." Instead, they are confronted by "arms mounted on a box" that wave back and forth like the tentacles of giant sea anemones. And they make noises straight out of a comic book: *Squooooonk,* and a "fireplug" spins half a turn; *screeeee,* a shoulder bends up and a forearm dips; *sssss,* a hand begins to spin.

The hand begins to spin? What better way to fasten bolts, one of the robot's most important jobs. In fact, a robot doesn't have a single hand; it has a whole tool chest of them. With its wrench hand, the robot can fasten bolts. With a paint-sprayer hand, it can paint. It also has a soldering-iron hand, a welding-torch hand, and a "gripper"—parallel jaws like those found on a pipe wrench or vise.

HERE COME THE ROBOTS

Even as late as the 1950's, there were no robots in factories. Now there are over ten thousand—mostly in Japan, the United States, and Western Europe. Spurred on by miniature computers, rising labor costs, and declining productivity, there may be as many as 200,000 robots by 1990—just in the United States alone.

These "steel-collar workers" are fast, efficient, and reliable. What's more, human laborers and their unions have welcomed their arrival. Robots have taken over the nastiest jobs in the factory—jobs that are dangerous, repetitive, and boring.

Even considering their many uses, most present-day factory robots are primitive compared to the robots in science fiction. They can't see, they can't hear, they have little or no sense of touch; except for their "arms," they can't move. They have little intelligence.

But these older robots will soon be replaced by a new generation of robots emerging from the laboratories. The new robots will have specialized vision, a sense of touch, "ears" so they can obey spoken commands, and wheels so they can move around. What is more, they will be smart enough to cope with the jumble of parts, the assembly-line changes, and the confusion often found in a modern factory.

Nevertheless, despite the robots' skills, what will be their long-term impact on people's lives? Will advanced industrial robots be a benefit or a threat? When a robot bumps a person off the assembly line, what happens to the person? What kind of products will "automated" factories of the future produce? And are worker robots confined to the factories, or can they also replace people in clerical jobs, in offices, and in the professions, such as medicine and law? Will their social impact be beneficial, as Aristotle foresaw, or will it be something quite different?

PRECURSORS TO MODERN ROBOTS

The history of worker robots is really the history of *automation* —the replacement of human or animal muscle by an automaton, or machine.

In 1509, a German knight known as Goetz von Berlichingen lost his hand in battle. An ingenious metalworker came up with one of the earliest prostheses, and what was probably history's first working robot hand. The hand was made of iron and was very heavy. It was fastened on to the knight's wrist with leather straps and had gears for the knight's fingers and thumb. The fingers were kept extended by springs; they could be flexed by ratchets and levers.

In the eighteenth and nineteenth centuries, after clocks had come into widespread use, scores of automata were produced with insides made of clocklike mechanisms of metal gears, springs, and wires. Other automata appeared, powered by metal drums. As the drums rotated, pegs on the drums activated the automata's machinery and made them appear very lifelike. Parlor guests of society's wealthy elite were delighted by mechanical servants that played the harpsichord, wrote letters, poured wine, scooped up dirt, and hammered nails.

The latter half of the eighteenth century ushered in the Industrial Revolution. Probably the key development with regard to automation came in the 1790's with the invention of the centrifugal governor by James Watt, a Scot. Watt invented the governor to regulate the speed of his other invention, the steam engine. When the engine began running too fast, the governor slowed it down. The governor actually gave the steam engine a primitive "self-awareness." It was the first application of the principle of *feedback:* With the governor, the engine could sense and correct deviations from a desired control setting.

During the next 150 years, machines grew more flexible in what they could do, and their materials and components became ever more advanced. Special-purpose machines began appearing in factories around the world. One type of machine could weld; another could paint. But these machines were not robots. They were built with only one wired-in program (list of functions), and that was all. If a factory needed a different function, it had to purchase a new machine.

A tremendous number of technical advances occurred preceding and during World War II. Out of the war came a new breed of machines that were numerically controlled, the NC Machines. Their functions could be represented as jumbles of multicolored wires fastened to a plugboard; as settings on *potentiometers* regulating voltage; or as patterns of holes punched into paper tapes. The NC Machines were remarkable because they were general-purpose. Depending on the instructions stored in their memory (the plugboard, potentiometer, or paper tape), they could weld, paint, or do a hundred other tasks.

Now robots were just around the corner. In the mid-1950's, George Devol, an inventor, patented several of his concepts for a "general-purpose computerized industrial machine whose functions can be varied according to the program stored in the machine's memory." In 1960, using Devol's ideas, the first industrial robot was built. In 1961, Unimation, the world's first manufacturer of industrial robots, built its first robot. Known as a Unimate, the robot went to General Motors for use in one of its automobile assembly plants.

When it first went into business, Unimation could only build and ship four robots a month. Its first robots had their functions stored on a metal drum "memory," and they were capable of only a limited number of tasks. Today, forty new Unimates emerge from the Unimation plant every month, and there are over seven thousand Unimates in action all over the world. Their punch cards show they've put in over 10 million hours on the job. Controlled by high-speed electronic computers, their capabilities are endless.

The most important single development since the appearance of the Unimate is the rise of Japan. The Japanese now have ten thousand robots working in factories, and another two thousand new ones are added to the work force every year.

In Japan both the government and large corporations are spending vast sums of money to develop new robots with more advanced senses and intelligence. Faced with an acute labor shortage and motivated by a desire to increase productivity and become preeminent in new, computer-related markets, the Japanese are making advances in robotics at an unprecedented rate.

COMPUTER CONTROL VERSUS HUMAN CONTROL

Two types of industrial "robots" have evolved since the 1950's. One type is controlled by a computer, the other is remotely controlled by a person. According to our definition, real robots must have senses and be computer-controlled. Few industrial robots as yet meet these rigid standards.

There are fewer remotely controlled machines—teleoperators or telecherics—and their technology is not as advanced as real robotics technology. Nevertheless, these machines, though few in number, have important jobs, such as conducting experiments with chemicals that are toxic or emit dangerous radiation.

Teleoperators were once operated by wires, gears, and levers, but since the 1940's, most of them have been powered by electricity. If the human operator is nearby—in the next room or behind a protective shielding—he or she can control the "teleop" by pushing buttons or moving special grippers, levers, knobs, and handles to generate an electrical signal. The signal travels along a wire to the teleop and activates its electric motors, causing the teleop to mimic the person's actions. Long-distance, remotely controlled teleops have also been used, especially in the space program. The only difference between a remotely controlled teleop on the next planet and one in the next room is that the former receives its signals by radio waves and the latter by electric cable.

ROBOT SKILLS AND ABILITIES

Since the 1950's a major controversy has arisen concerning the skills and abilities that should be built into industrial robots. Many industry engineers and most scientists feel robots will be significantly improved by making them smarter and by adding rudimentary senses—sight, hearing, and touch—to make them more aware of their environment. Yet adding these features is extremely difficult and will make the robots more complicated and expensive.

Most industrial robots presently in use have neither sensory devices nor advanced intelligence. Once programmed, they follow the same set of instructions over and over, with little or no feedback from the outside world. This keeps them simple and relatively cheap. Nevertheless, they are amazingly precise and reliable. As one major user puts it: "I don't need smart, seeing robots. My robots do the job. . . ."

ROBOTS IN THE LABOR FORCE—A SURVEY

Most Unimate robots cost from $30,000 to $60,000 apiece. But in comparison with other, larger robots, they're cheap. Cincinnati Milacron, Unimation's biggest competitor, makes a robot called the T^3 that costs almost $70,000. A Swedish manufacturer, ASEA, makes one that costs $100,000. Yet in spite of these large price tags, robots are in great demand, and all forecasts call for that demand to grow rapidly over the next ten to twenty years.

In 1960 there were no industrial robots. In 1981, there were more than twenty thousand industrial robots worldwide. According to some estimates, by 1990, as many as 200,000 robots will be at work, and industrial users will be spending over a billion dollars on new robots each year. According to William

Park, a robot expert at SRI International in California, "the great robot race is on."

Why is the future of industrial robots so rosy? There are several reasons. First, due to the miniaturization of computers and new manufacturing techniques, the cost of robots has been dropping dramatically. A $50,000 robot today may cost less than $10,000 by 1990.

Second, in spite of their high cost, robots are relatively cheap in comparison to the skyrocketing cost of human labor. Over the last twenty years, the average salary for a factory worker has gone from $3.80 an hour to over $16.00 an hour. During that same period, the total cost of a robot-hour (including installation, maintenance, depreciation, and energy) has increased from $4.00 to only $4.80. A robot can work a full three shifts (twenty-four hours) a day. It never shows up late or hung over. It has no personal problems. It doesn't complain about working conditions. It never takes a coffee break. It rarely gets sick. (Unimate robots, for example, stay healthy over 98 percent of the time.)

The robot will do the same dull, dangerous, and dirty work over and over again, day in and day out—until it is reprogrammed, usually a matter of two to four weeks. Then, instead of being a welder, the robot becomes a painter or an assembler. By contrast, a human worker who must be retrained might take several months or even years to unlearn old habits and master new skills.

HUMAN-ROBOT TEAMS

For certain types of jobs, robots are better than their human counterparts: They're faster, more efficient, more precise, and more reliable.

On the other hand, despite robots' advantages in some areas, in most jobs humans are vastly superior. This is especially true for assembly jobs—jobs that involve recognizing and matching parts, a task at which robots are notoriously bad.

But robots and humans needn't always work alone. In fact, in many instances, companies acquire robots and create human-robot teams to do certain jobs. In this way, the humans and robots can pool their talents and offset each other's weaknesses. Human workers can cope with the unexpected, can deal with situations where there is inadequate information, and can apply common sense. Meanwhile, robots can handle jobs that are beyond the human workers' strength, ability, or endurance.

How do human and robot workers get along? In the beginning the human workers often fear and distrust the robots. Later, after they have been working side by side for a period of time, an uncanny sense of camaraderie develops—at least on the part of the humans. For example, in most plants, the robot workers acquire a nickname after only a short time on the job. At a GE plant, for example, the human workers named their robot co-worker "Rex." One morning, a few months after Rex's arrival, the plant manager was walking by the robot and noticed something tacked to his side. It was Rex's membership card in the local steelworkers union.

ROBOT LIMITATIONS

A company thinking about adding robots to its work force has to consider many different issues. For example, if the company's products never, or only rarely, change, the company probably needs a special-purpose machine rather than a programmable robot.

Another consideration for the company is how much the plant and manufacturing procedures must be modified if robots are acquired. Industrial robots can only work in factories that have been prepared for them. New equipment has to be added, parts have to be retooled, the imprecision and disorder that humans put up with must be eliminated. According to some experts, robotization of a factory might cost as much as ten times the cost of the robots themselves.

When the robot finally arrives, there is a long period while it is being taught and debugged so that it will run correctly. And if things are not coordinated perfectly, all of the preparation is worthless. Most factory robots are still sightless and lack a sense of touch—they're "blind grabbers," reaching mindlessly toward where a part should be. As a result, much effort goes into getting parts *exactly* into the right position where a robot can handle them. This need for absolute precision is illustrated by an example of a robot handling a transistor radio. Its job is simple: pick up the radio. But if the radio is slightly out of place, the robot might close its grippers around an exposed transistor instead of the radio's metal frame. The result is a crushed transistor. Unless a human supervisor is looking over the robot's "shoulder," no one is any wiser. After all, the robot doesn't know it has done anything wrong.

THE NEAR FUTURE:
A NEW GENERATION OF ROBOTS

It is expensive for companies to make their factory operations ultra-precise so that they can safely employ "handicapped" robots of low intelligence and little sensory ability. Also, each time the robots begin a new job, they have to be laboriously trained by leading them through perhaps dozens of positions.

Furthermore, as long as robots are so expensive, only the largest companies will be able to afford them. Most robots already installed in factories are only equipped to weld and paint large, high-volume products, like automobiles. Few industrial robots can handle assembly—picking up parts and fastening them together. Yet from 75–95 percent of United States industrial production is composed of *batch manufactur-*

ing—assembling components to make a relatively small number of finished products of a given style or design. Surprisingly, this is even the case in the automobile industry, the largest employer of industrial robots, where small-parts batch assembly accounts for more than 90 percent of the parts in most cars.

Fortunately, help is on the way. A new generation of robots is leaving the laboratory and entering the factory. The new robots are cheaper and smarter than their predecessors. Their intelligence and their senses—vision, touch, and, sometimes, hearing—will enable them to work on the production line assembling and inspecting small batches of products from skis to pharmaceuticals, from skateboards to automobile dashboards.

FACTORY ROBOTS THAT "SEE"

It is easy to attach a robot to a TV camera so it can "see." What is hard is teaching the robot to understand *what* it sees, to recognize patterns. But recognizing patterns takes an enormous amount of calculation, and for this the robot needs an immensely fast computer. Until recently, these computers were prohibitively expensive. After all, manufacturers are not likely to buy a $200,000 computer to get a $50,000 robot to do a minimum-wage job.

Despite the obstacles, however, great progress is being made in giving robots vision. The new computers on a chip, for example, can be wired together into an array of "brain cells" that produce lightning-fast vision calculations yet are still relatively cheap.

One of the most interesting "seeing" robots is Battelle Laboratories' micro-mouse, a little robot that uses infrared detectors for eyes and six computer chips for intelligence and memory. The mouse shows an amazing ability to learn maze-like passageways by trial and error and by inductive reasoning.

Battelle is grooming the mouse to act as a guide and carry messages back and forth inside underground mines or inside labyrinthine networks of ducts and pipes.

FACTORY ROBOTS THAT "FEEL"

A sense of touch can be a crucial trait in advanced robots. In many cases, a robot needs to know how hard its gripper "hand" is squeezing something. If the hand doesn't squeeze hard enough, it doesn't pick up the object. If it squeezes too hard, it will crush it. The hand also needs to know when it is touching the object, or it might keep reaching for it and knock it off the conveyor belt.

It is fairly easy to install microswitches, strain gauges, thermometers, and other devices on a robot hand that will improve its sense of touch. Using these devices, the robot will be able to touch objects and sense heat, cold, weight, pressure, texture, and vibration. But it is much more difficult to get the robot to understand *what* it is touching.

Again, progress is being made. For example, Draper Laboratories in Cambridge, Massachusetts, has developed a gripper with a tactile (touch) sense. If a machine part is being jammed or wedged instead of going into a hole cleanly, the robot equipped with this hand can jiggle the part or apply pressure in a different direction. Using this new hand, a sightless robot can assemble the seventeen parts of an automobile alternator in only 2 minutes and 42 seconds.

Some scientists speculate that robots equipped with advanced vision and touch will someday have enough hand-to-eye and hand-to-hand coordination that they will come equipped with twenty arms—each with telescoping forearms and rotating wrists. Such robots would be extremely useful in assembling different items, such as motors and machine tools. And they would be fast. Present-day robots like Unimation's PUMA can move their single arm over ten feet in a single second.

The mobile robot Cart and its inventor, Hans Moravec. The Cart is an early version of a mobile, seeing, underwater explorer robot.   *Stantord University*

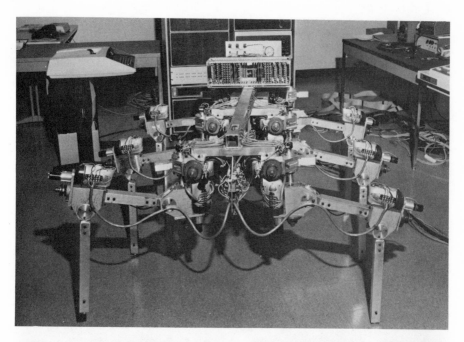

The OSU Hexapod, a six-legged, walking robot developed by scientists at Ohio State University in Columbus, Ohio. *Ohio State University*

Most working robots in the United States are employed in the automobile industry. These robots weld car frames, spray-paint car bodies, inspect, assemble, and stack car parts, and perform many other chores. *Unimation Inc. and* Robotics Today

Unimation PUMAs are members of a new generation of industrial robots. Some PUMAs have been outfitted with advanced computers, others with computer vision and a sense of touch. The small (120-pound) robot can only lift 5 pounds, but it has enough strength to assemble 90 percent of all automobile parts. The PUMA in this picture is installing a light bulb in back of the instrument panel on a car dashboard.

Unimation Inc. and General Motors Corporation

These "seeing" robots are transferring newly assembled calculators from one moving conveyor belt to another.   *Texas Instruments Inc.*

Theseus, the robot "mouse," is programmed to find his way through complicated mazes. *Courtesy of David Ziffer, Robert Matz, Scott Pector, and Irving Moy*

Although the RCV-150 is a remote-controlled vehicle (via underwater cable) and not a true robot, it nevertheless has many robotic features, including a manipulator arm and TV-camera "vision."

Hydro Products, Inc.

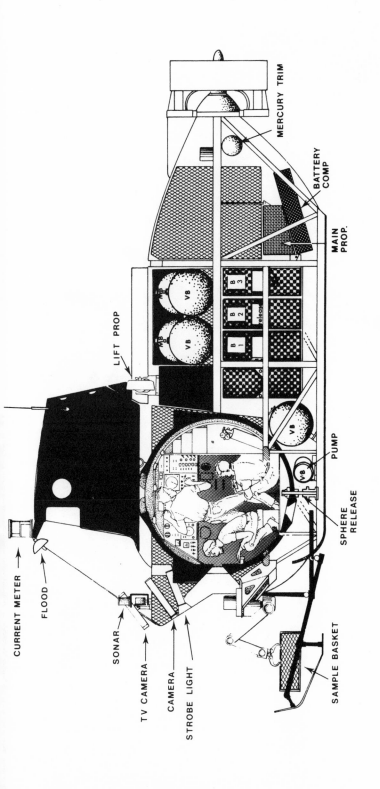

CURRENT METER →

FLOOD

SONAR

TV CAMERA

CAMERA

STROBE LIGHT

SAMPLE BASKET

LIFT PROP

MERCURY TRIM

BATTERY COMP

MAIN PROP.

VB

VB

B 1

B 2

B 3

release

VB

VB

PUMP

SPHERE RELEASE

SYNTACTIC FOAM

MB_a MAIN BALLAST, AIR

MAIN BALLAST TANK

¦B¦ BATTERY

VB VARIABLE BALLAST

The *Alvin* is not a true robot, since it is operated by human pilots on board. However, it has a remote manipulator (a robot arm) and a growing number of sensors, including sonar and TV and solid-state cameras.   *Woods Hole Oceanographic Institution*

The Mars Viking Lander is part robot, part remote-controlled vehicle. Its onboard computers record and interpret information generated from its experiments and from its various sensors. In addition, it is controlled by human operators on Earth via radio signals. *NASA and the Jet Propulsion Laboratory*

This prototype of the Mars Rover is a seeing, mobile, computer-controlled robot with a manipulator arm for gathering soil and rock samples from the Martian surface.

Jet Propulsion Laboratory

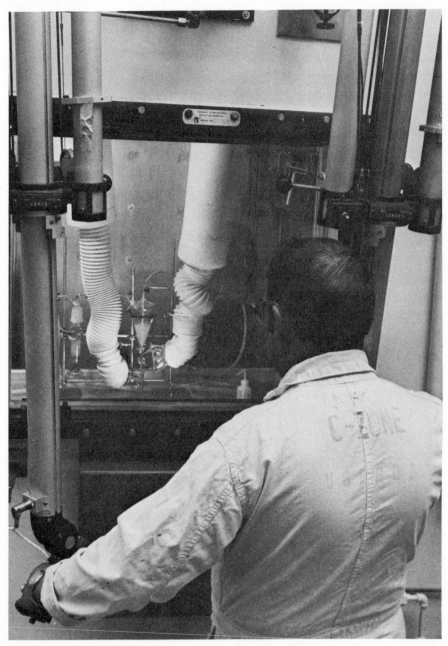

A human technician is operating a *master/slave manipulator* to handle dangerous radioactive substances.

EXPLORER ROBOTS

There are many different types of explorer vehicles. Some are true robots. Others are not, but are evolving in that direction. We'll take a look at both kinds in this chapter.

Machines that carry their human operators inside often have sensors but no intelligence. They are operated directly (as opposed to remotely) by human beings.

There are also *master/slave manipulators* and remote-controlled vehicles. These are also referred to as teleoperators and telecherics. Newer machines in this class have a certain level of intelligence (or onboard, decision-making computers) and no human occupants. Instead, their human operators control them and "talk" to them from remote locations. Planetary explorer robots, like the Viking spacecraft that landed on the surface of Mars, are examples of teleoperators that (with their sensors and computers) are also robots.

Next, there are the fully computer-controlled robots. These robots, just now being developed, will have more independence and intelligence than all of the other robots. Coupled with computer vision, hearing, and tactile sensors, they will be able to explore areas dangerous to humans, protect themselves from accidents, conduct experiments, perform construction and manufacturing, and store and relay information back to human beings. The mobile Mars Rover robot and the tiny computerized mice robots are examples of these new intelligent robots.

And lastly, there are the *telepresences,* advanced teleoperators that combine computer control with advanced sensory and motor capabilities. They can give a remote human operator the feeling that he or she actually *is* the teleop—deep in outer space, in a mine miles underground, or on a work platform thousands of feet beneath the ocean's surface.

UNDERSEA EXPLORERS

It is a world straight out of someone's fantasy—or nightmare. Chimneys rise out of a hardened lava floor and spew hot black clouds of watery, mineral-laden smoke. Tiny, scurrying crabs overrun foot-long, scarlet-red clams with corroded white shells. Weird dandelionlike creatures are whipped back and forth by currents of warm water, anchored only by gossamer filaments of thread. Enormous blood-red worms wriggle and wave from the tops of a forest of plasticlike tubes.

Through this eerie, darkened world moves a robotlike machine, raking the worms, the chimneys, the dandelionlike creatures, and the clams with bright white light from headlamps mounted on one of its arms. Its other arm works ceaselessly, grabbing rocks, collecting the delicate sea creatures, taking temperature readings, and sampling the seawater and the sediment of the sea floor.

The site, located in the Pacific Ocean, is known as the Mid-Oceanic Ridge. It is part of the 40,000-mile-long undersea mountain range and rift system that runs underneath all four of the world's oceans. The underwater vehicle is the Deep

Submergence Research Vehicle (DSRV) *Alvin,* really a combination teleoperator and submarine. It is occupied by a pilot
and two scientific researchers.

Over the years since it was created, the *Alvin* has become
less like a submarine and more like a robot. It has a sophisticated group of sensors and instruments that measure everything
from temperature and water velocity to the concentration of
bacteria and plant life in the water. Its two arms operate lab
equipment, take samples, and photograph the undersea world
it is exploring. Recently, sophisticated new vision sensors have
been developed, including a color video camera that the *Alvin*
can set up on a platform on the ocean floor. Three tiny
electronic CCD chips translate the images of undersea objects
into patterns of binary bits (like those stored in a computer).
These digitized images can be viewed and taped inside the
Alvin. Later, a computer can enhance and manipulate these
images, much the way computers manipulate and enhance
pictures of planets taken by robot space probes.

The *Alvin,* now almost twenty years old, is merely the
forerunner of a whole new generation of undersea robots.
Since it is operated by humans inside the vehicle, it has no
independence, or "intelligence," of its own.

However, new undersea vehicles are being developed that
carry no humans onboard. One type is equipped with television cameras and operated, via a long cable, by humans in
another craft, either above the vehicle or in a ship on the
surface. For example, the RCV-150 and the RCV-225 are two
remote-controlled vehicles that are used extensively in the
construction, inspection, and maintenance of offshore oil-
drilling platforms located all around the world. The RCV-150
looks like a large metallic eyeball. To begin an operation, the
RCV-150 is placed in a cage, known either as a "launcher" or a
"garage." The vehicle, inside its cage, is lowered into the
water. At the desired depth, the RCV-150 takes off from its
garage under the power of small but strong electrohydraulic

motors. The vehicle has a TV camera onboard that transmits pictures back to a TV monitor on the surface ship. The RCV-150's human operators watch the monitor and use a joystick and a control station to steer the vehicle through the water. The vehicle also has four extremely bright work lights and a manipulator (arm).

For the first time, using the RCV-150 and the RCV-225, engineers and technicians on the surface can monitor and guide the work being done underwater by human divers. The vehicles can also help surface "dive" managers monitor the divers' physical condition. Human divers, working hundreds of feet underwater, are subject to tremendous emotional and physical stress. When a dive manager watching the television screen notices a diver showing fatigue or confusion, he can have him or her take a break.

THE GROWING IMPORTANCE
OF UNDERSEA ROBOTS

Why is there such an interest in undersea robots? Here are some of the reasons.

Undersea research. Marine biologists can study underwater animal and plant life; geologists, by exploring the ocean floor, can learn a great deal about the formation and evolution of the earth's surface.

Mineral prospecting and mining. We face, over the next ten to twenty years, a growing global scarcity of all kinds of minerals and other vital raw materials. Huge deposits of minerals, such as manganese and phosphorus, have been discovered along the ocean floor. Now techniques need to be developed to mine these minerals and aid our search for more minerals.

Undersea manufacturing plants. It is practical to locate factories underwater, close to the site of important raw materials.

Oil production. As known oil deposits diminish, undersea oil prospecting and the construction and maintenance of undersea oil platforms are becoming increasingly more important. Already, 30 percent of all the world's oil is produced offshore. In another few years, this figure will jump to 50 percent.

Harvesting the ocean. Crops such as seaweed and other vegetation make valuable animal fodder and will be used more and more to supplement human diet.

Ocean thermal energy conversion. This is a new technology that utilizes the significant difference in temperature between the solar-heated surface water and the icy water of the ocean depths to create electricity. As part of this process, long intake tubes, lowered 1,000–3,000 feet into the sea, will draw cold water up to the surface.

The new robots being developed now will combine human-like dexterity and intelligence with their own superior strength and endurance. They will be ideal as workers in undersea factories and for maintaining underwater equipment. Equipped with special underwater sensory devices, they will do the exploring, prospecting, mining, and building necessary to open up the vast store of riches that awaits us on the floor of the world's oceans.

OUTER-SPACE ROBOTS

Louis L'Amour, the best-selling author of novels about the American West, has called outer space "the next American frontier." Our Mars Viking Landers, our planetary flyby spacecraft such as Voyagers 1 and 2, the Space Shuttle, and other Earth orbiters are only the first steps of a long-term effort to explore, colonize, and industrialize space.

Currently, the top national priority is to industrialize space rather than explore it. It is easy to see why. For many reasons, outer space is an ideal environment for the manufacture of many products. The vacuum found in space, the extreme cold, the absence of dust particles, bacteria, or other airborne impurities, and the lack of gravity make it possible to produce "perfect" crystals, magnets, and lenses, for example.

Unfortunately, many of these same features make space extremely inhospitable for human beings. The question then arises, Do we really need to go there? The answer is yes. With a rapidly growing world population, modernizing societies, and increasingly scarce Earth-based natural resources, we are forced to look elsewhere. Outer space is a necessary alternative.

But since space is filled with hazards and enormous risks to people's lives and well-being, what is really needed is for us to develop a new generation of machines that can take our place and perform many of the needed tasks. Eventually, huge manufacturing complexes will be operated in space, on planets, and on planetary moons. These factories will be constructed and maintained almost entirely by robots and other computerized machines. Only small numbers of human supervisors and technicians will be needed to oversee the entire operation.

What types of robots will be needed? Outer-space robots have been around for years, since all spacecraft not operated directly by human beings are, in a sense, robots. They are complicated machines that can perform delicate operations, are mobile, and have sensory organs that allow them to see and hear things far beyond the range of human senses. And many of these vehicles have onboard computers, which give them a certain level of intelligence, decision-making powers, and independence.

Most spacecraft that leave Earth are special-purpose robots, with only a single mission in mind. The most numerous robots are Earth-orbiting communication satellites that send and receive messages across all parts of the planet. Other types include military and "observer" satellites, such as those used to study and record the earth's weather and climatic patterns. The Soviet Union has launched unmanned robot spaceships that have brought supplies to cosmonauts circling the earth in a space station.

The newest satellite robot will be a space telescope, orbiting the earth well outside its obscuring atmosphere and capable of seeing stars—and even planets—that are fifty times dimmer than those currently seen through Earth's largest land-based telescopes.

Not all robots are Earth satellites, of course. The most famous robots to date are the planetary and interplanetary explorer robots. These include America's Viking robots, which landed on the surface of Mars, relayed pictures of Mars back to Earth, and scooped up soil with long mechanical arms and tested the soil in an onboard laboratory to see if any plants or animals were present. The Soviets, too, have explorer robots. The Russian Lunokhod 1 was similar to the Viking robots. A mobile robot, it landed on the moon, crawled across the surface, and, like the Viking, took soil samples and relayed them back to scientists on Earth. Soon a new Soviet space robot will land on Venus and perform similar experiments.

There are also "planetary flyby" explorer robots, like the Voyager series. These robots fly through the solar system from planet to planet and use high-resolution cameras, which produce extremely sharp pictures that are relayed back to Earth, where they are "decoded" and enhanced by Earth-based computers.

A whole new generation of outer-space robots is now on the drawing boards. The robots come in all sizes and shapes, but the focus is on two major types: robots designed to work in the airless vacuum of space itself; and others that will be used on another planet, on a space station or work platform, or on an asteroid.

As early as 1966, NASA was testing the Space Taxi, a spacecraft resembling an undersea vehicle like the *Alvin*. The Taxi, which is designed to be flown by one person, has several manipulators, or arms, to enable it to do construction and repair or maintenance jobs in space. New versions of the Taxi are being designed by NASA and by private corporations. Some are computer-controlled and can operate without a human pilot. For example, scientists at the Marshall Space Flight Center in Huntsville, Alabama, are developing a robot that will launch itself from the space shuttle, locate an ailing satellite, and repair it.

Another early NASA space vehicle was the Space Horse, also known as the Maneuvering Work Platform. The Horse could be ridden, like the space car used by astronauts on the Apollo Moon mission. It had three strong arms that allowed an astronaut to carry and manipulate heavy objects and perform maneuvers an astronaut would find difficult to do in a space suit or on a planet with especially low or high gravity.

One of the newest—and most exciting—outer-space robots is the mobile Mars Rover, an independent explorer robot powered by a radioactive thermal generator (RTG). Scientists on Earth will be able to control the Rover, but it will also have onboard microcomputers to give it enough intelligence and memory to be able to "recognize" unusual opportunities and dangerous situations. Working Rovers have already been constructed at the Jet Propulsion Laboratory in Pasadena, California. These prototype Rovers can sense their environment and manipulate tools, instruments, and other objects almost as well as human beings can.

It is crucial that a robot like the Rover be independent, since it takes up to forty minutes for a signal to reach Mars from Earth. This long transmission time would greatly hamper the Rover's ability to conduct experiments and explore the surface of the planet safely and productively—*if* the Rover were totally dependent on signals sent from scientists on Earth. Instead, the Rover has been designed to be independent and only asks the scientists for directions for major undertakings.

A prototype model of the Rover moves at a rate of one meter per minute. It has special jointed legs and "loopwheels" that permit it to move over very rough, boulder- and crater-strewn terrain, and climb or descend slopes up to 30 degrees.

The Rover has stereo vision, using twin cameras mounted on the front. In addition, it has a laser range finder that locates nearby obstacles. Once its eyes have located obstacles, its computer brain considers this, then charts the least hazardous course around the obstacles and on to the Rover's destination.

The Rover also has limited "hand-eye" coordination and uses its cameras to guide its pincer and gripper hands to sample objects found on the planet's surface. Work is being done now to enable it to grab and manipulate moving objects. This would make a Roverlike robot useful in docking, maintenance, and repair operations on an orbiting spacecraft like the Space Shuttle.

Currently, the Mars mission where the Rover will be deployed has been postponed to 1999. In the meantime, Rover-like, intelligent manipulator robots are being developed for a number of outer-space and Earth-based tasks. For example, there is a lot of interest in shifting many industrial and manufacturing activities to outer space. Activities will include the construction of large antennas, space stations, solar-power stations, and "space factories," also known as orbiting manu-facturing modules (OMM). Robots will also be used to transport radioactive and other hazardous waste materials to outer space.

Roverlike robots are also being converted into robots to aid the handicapped. For example, a voice-controlled robotic wheelchair for quadriplegics is being tested. The robot has a manipulator arm that moves and picks up objects at the operator's voice command.

TELEPRESENCE

For the past twenty years, the major thrust of research and development has been in the area of computer-controlled robots, like the Rover. Now, once again, there is renewed interest in remotely controlled vehicles—teleoperators that humans control and computers assist.

Most remote-control robotic work has been performed as part of the United States space program. For example, the Jet Propulsion Laboratory has designed a robot arm and hand from an astronaut's space suit. The arm and hand, attached to a computer, can be placed aboard a spaceship and launched into outer space. Then a person on Earth can put on an exact duplicate of the arm and hand and, watching a TV screen, can maneuver the spaceship arm and hand to pick up objects, handle tools, conduct experiments, and operate the spaceship's controls. Interestingly, by watching the screen and operating the arm and hand on Earth, one gets the uncanny feeling of actually being in outer space.

According to many scientists, it is this feeling of being there that gives remotely controlled teleoperators such great potential. Marvin Minsky, a scientist at MIT, recently called for a crash program to develop a new generation of ultrasophisticated, remotely controlled "teleops." They would be designed so as to give their human operator the sensation of being electronically transported to where the teleop was working—to be "in the teleop's shoes." Minsky calls this advanced remote-control teleop a telepresence.

A telepresence, in the form of an advanced manipulator arm, has already been invented and is now being tested by NASA. Once in space, the telepresence, controlled by a human operator on Earth, could make repairs outside a spaceship, make adjustments to external equipment, and load and unload cargo or scientific instruments.

The telepresence differs from NASA's older teleop arm in two key respects: Inside its body are advanced microcomputers and sensors that give it a remarkable awareness of its outer-space environment. As the telepresence arm and hand work, they automatically sense forces—pressure, weight, resistance, and so on—that are digitized and radioed back to Earth, where they are duplicated on a manipulator arm being operated in the control center. The signals from outer space are then translated into electricity and boosted until they are strong enough to drive tiny electric motors that pull cables on the control center's arm and hands. In this way, the human operator on Earth can be made to feel, almost instantaneously, the same forces that are acting on the telepresence in space.

A hand and an arm are only the beginning. Minsky envisions sending an entire telepresence body into space. To operate the telepresence, a person on Earth wears a work suit fitted with thousands of tiny receivers that pick up the sensory data being sent from the telepresence. In this way, the person can stay at home and still perform his or her work. Wearing the work suit and watching a TV screen, he can move about, raise or lower his arms, make a fist, or whatever. And the telepresence—far away—will duplicate these actions.

For example, if the telepresence is assembling a solar-energy panel in orbit around Earth, the human operator will sense the vacuum that surrounds the telepresence, the coldness of space, and the brightness of direct, unshielded sunlight. Yet these sensations will be dampened so as not to be harmful or painful. Similarly, if the human has the telepresence grasp a tool, he will feel the pressure, the weight, even the temperature of the tool in his own empty hand.

Telepresences could be used in any area where the working conditions were hazardous. They could be used to supervise a team of computer-controlled robots building lunar-based laboratories, telescopes, or manufacturing plants. They could be used to monitor underwater robots that would drill, mine, and farm the ocean floor. They could be used to fight fires and deactivate bombs. They could be used to service orbiting satellites. Perhaps even more exciting, surgeons could use miniature telepresences—microscopic, robotic arms and tools —to conduct extremely delicate surgery. The small telepresences could enter and perform surgery inside a person's brain, his eyes, and his blood vessels' narrowest passages.

8
ROBOTS IN
THE CLASSROOM

The Union County Career Center near Charlotte, North Carolina, is a very busy place. Eleventh and twelfth graders from the four county high schools work at the center part-time to develop vocational skills such as metalworking and electronics. Each year when the tenth graders come to the Center to learn about its activities, they need a guide to show them around.

The guide is Unicorn 1, a radio-controlled teleoperator built by the Center's electronics class with the aid of their instructor. Building it was a big project, so the students worked up to it gradually. In earlier semesters they worked on such items as a digital alarm clock, a digital tachometer, and a radio-operated model school bus. The class even built two predecessors to Unicorn 1. The first was Gus the Talking School Bus. The students installed an FM radio receiver and speakers in Gus's grille. Gus, dressed up with a huge baseball cap on his roof, eyes painted on the windshield and a smile across his grille, makes tours around North Carolina promoting school-bus safety.

The more immediate predecessor to Unicorn 1 was a soccer-ball-sized Turtle robot that zips around the classroom floor under the control of a microcomputer the students programmed.

And the students' plans for Unicorn 1? First they would like to get rid of the cumbersome wires leading to its battery and control panel and make it fully radio-controlled. Next they want to install a microcomputer brain and program it to operate on its own.

PROGRAMMING A ROBOT ARM

In this book you've seen some of the big robots that work in factories. They are really just robotic arms. Still, some of the largest ones weigh several thousand pounds. Many of the robot manufacturers are now building lighter arms. However, even these small industrial robots can cost several thousand dollars, which makes them too expensive for classroom use.

But new, less expensive robot arms are on the way. Hobby Robots Company, in Lilburn, Georgia, has developed a robot arm, a robot hand, and a robot shoulder. The parts can be easily put together and cost less than a thousand dollars.

If your class is interested in a complete robot arm that is already assembled, it might consider the MiniMover 5 from Microbot, in Menlo Park, California. A relatively inexpensive robot (costing less than two thousand dollars), it is a five-jointed arm with a positioning accuracy of 0.013 inches, and a top speed of up to 12 inches a second. It can lift weights up to 8 ounces. The robot is built of plastic and aluminum and is controlled by cables attached to a joint pulley and stepping motors mounted on the robot's base. You can hook it up to a small computer and program it in assembly language or ARMBASIC, a dialect of BASIC.

There is a wide range of experiments you can try with the MiniMover 5. You can write artificial-intelligence programs to teach the robot how to pick up and assemble different-shaped blocks. You can load chess, backgammon, Monopoly, and other board-game programs into the computer and program MiniMover 5 to move the game pieces around the board. You can program it to simulate the big industrial arms in automated construction and assembly. You can create an unlimited variety of computer art by programming MiniMover 5's gripper to pick up different brushes and felt-tip pens and draw pictures on a blank page or canvas.

ROBOTS THAT TEACH POWERFUL IDEAS

For the last fifteen years there has been a project under way at MIT's Artificial Intelligence Laboratory and in Boston city schools to see how we go about learning math and other subjects. The name of the program is LOGO, from the Greek word *logos,* which combines the ideas of speech, thought, words, and reason. LOGO has attempted to apply some of the techniques discovered in robotics and artificial-intelligence research to improve young people's learning skills and to give them a clearer picture of the ways in which they learn.

Learning some things is easy; learning others is difficult. This ability to learn a subject is called *aptitude.* We have different *aptitudes* for different subjects, from shooting a basketball to playing a musical instrument. One of the most important aptitudes we can have is for arithmetic and mathematics. In our modern, technological society, a high aptitude for mathematics is almost essential. Most of us have an "on-off," or binary feeling about math—either we "get it" or we don't. Unfortunately, most of us feel that we don't.

The teachers involved in LOGO believe that the reason most of us do so miserably in math and find it so difficult and painful is *not* because we're not "brains." The real culprits, they feel, are the traditional methods used to teach math. How do *you* do math? You use a pencil and a piece of paper. And how do you learn math? You drill: The teacher and the textbook keep feeding you new problems—word problems, equations, diagrams, and graphs—and, with a few examples and hints from the teacher, you try to solve them.

At LOGO, both the methods and the technology for learning math are quite different. There, teachers look at mathematics as a language, a language that classroom experience indicates most of us can acquire. In place of the pencil and paper, students use the computer—more accurately, the computerized robot, or Turtle.

Turtle robots are circular, wheeled circuit boxes, about a foot in diameter, with a big, clear, Plexiglas "Turtle hump," or dome, on top. Turtles are wired to a small computer complete with typewriter keys to give them their commands.

Turtles can be programmed using various Turtle commands, such as FORWARD, RIGHT, LEFT, and END. Turtles can also draw. When you type in PENDOWN, the Turtle lowers a colored marker to the floor underneath its belly. Then, when you order the Turtle to go forward, or turn, it draws a picture.

One of the main goals in LOGO is to teach young people what is known as Turtle geometry. This is really ordinary geometry, but instead of having to spend most of your time using a pencil, a compass, a protractor, and an eraser (for all of your mistakes), you program the Turtle and get it to draw the shapes for you. Then you can concentrate on how to create new shapes rather than on the mechanical part of making your shapes look "pretty" or "neat."

When a Turtle behaves oddly and doesn't do what you want, this means it has a "bug"—an error—in its program. In most math classes, when a student turns in a solution to a problem, it is marked as either "wrong" or "right"—there's nothing in between. In LOGO, on the other hand, there is no such thing as

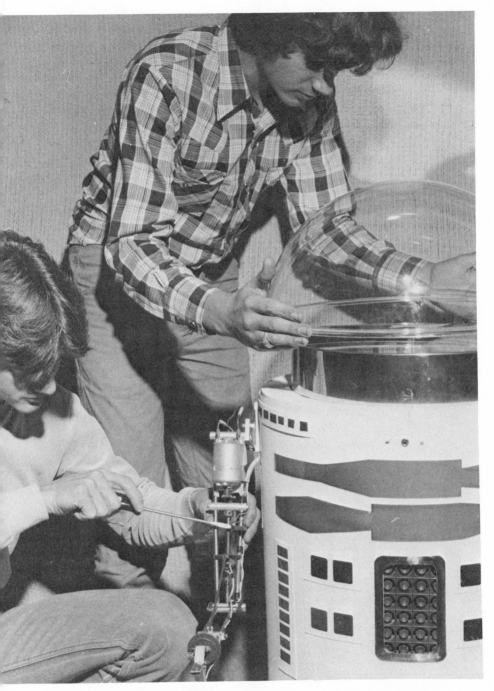

Robot builders Eddie Cook (*left*) and Scott Carter are putting the final touches on Unicorn I, the robot they and their classmates built as part of their robotics course at the Union County Career Center.   *James A. Gupton, Jr.*

Students can use a classroom computer to program the MiniMover 5 robot arm. The arm is small and lightweight, but it can be programmed to act like the robot arms used in factories.

Microbot

D. J. Reynolds and an early, partly assembled version of his "Electromechanical Household Helper." In this picture, Reynolds is operating the robot by remote control in order to test its steering and its motorized wheels.

D. J. Reynolds

Reggie I looks like a make-believe robot from a Hollywood movie. Actually he is a real working robot, complete with two computer brains, speech synthesis, and computer vision. *Ken D. Davis and General Development Company*

BORIS HANDroid is a chess-playing automaton with a robot arm, who can move his own chess pieces and remove your pieces from the board when he captures them. If you beat BORIS, his arm will come telescoping out, and, like a good sport, he'll shake your hand.
Applied Concepts, Inc.

Jonathan Kaplan is working on one of his homemade robots. Jonathan built seven robots in a small laboratory in his bedroom.
Jonathan T. and Flora Kaplan

The ET-2 looks like a robotic ashtray, but it is really a robot "shell." To turn the ET-2 into a true working robot, you need to add a battery, a microcomputer, plus sensors to gather information to feed to the computer brain.   *Lour Control*

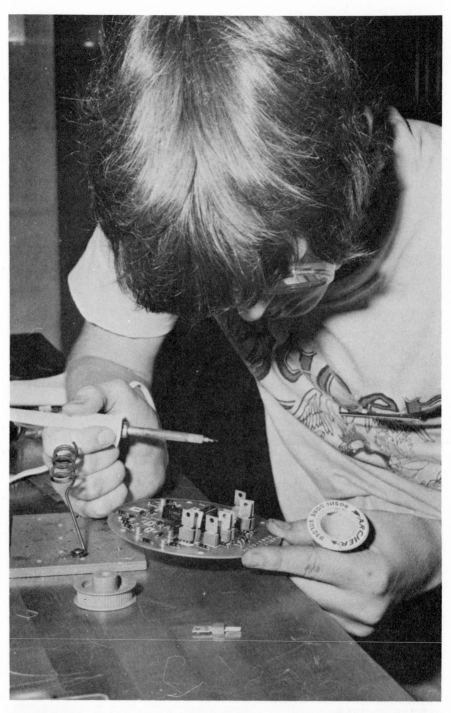

Richard Voss is soldering electronic components onto the circuit board of the Turtle robot he is building.

James A. Gupton, Jr.

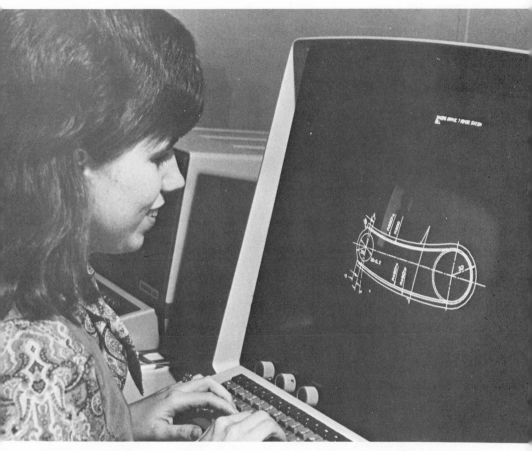

This woman is using a computer to design a new machine part. In the future, people will use computers and robots to design and manufacture most new products.

Control Data Corporation

Many types of dangerous, dehumanizing jobs might best be left to robots. Here a robot is dunking a white-hot machine part into a cooling liquid bath.   *Unimation Inc.*

"wrong." Instead there are programs that are gradually *de-bugged* until they work.

You get to see this debugging process in action by watching the Turtle zip back and forth across the floor and by talking about it with your classmates. You and your friends can work together, experimenting with the Turtle, electronically insert-ing and deleting commands, until you get it to do what you want. In this way, you are participating fully in the learning process. And, with help from your classmates and teacher, you are discovering many of the basic principles of geometry as you go. The process is spontaneous; it is not contrived as part of the teacher's preprogrammed lesson plan. Very often the students surprise the teacher with geometric principles they have discov-ered that are just as new to the teacher as to the students.

For the students in the LOGO lab, Turtle geometry (and even mathematics) is just the beginning. As the class progresses, the students graduate from the real-world robot Turtles to other turtles simulated as little circular "blips" on the computer picture screen. After learning math, students move into other subjects, such as physics. On the way, they acquire many things that they will take with them when they leave LOGO.

One of the most important skills they will leave with is the ability to see *how* they learn and the ability to improve the way they learn. Artificial-intelligence and robotics research have made significant advances in getting machines to think and learn. But perhaps their most significant contribution will be to teach people better ways of thinking and learning.

Once mastered, improved methods of thinking, problem solving, and learning can be applied in picking up many different skills in all areas of life. In the LOGO classroom, students and teachers have developed *human* programs (like computer programs) to learn skills as diverse as riding a unicycle, walking on stilts, and juggling.

Many people used to feel that the process of learning is

mysterious. But Seymour Papert, LOGO's founder and director, feels that the way we learn can be described very easily—as simple programs. If we know what these programs are, we can abandon the old method of trial-and-error and make learning quicker and easier.

WELCOME TO ROBOT-AIDED INSTRUCTION (RAI)

Computers have been used in classrooms for almost thirty years. Educational computing, known as Computer-Assisted Instruction (CAI) has focused on programmed drills and, to a lesser extent, on computer games and simulations—for example, conducting a chemistry experiment using simulated radioactive materials.

With the rapidly declining expenses of desk-top computers, schools are acquiring them by the tens of thousands. And now that robots and robot kits are appearing and are also becoming less expensive, teachers are beginning to use them in the classroom along with the computers. Basically, two types of computerized robots are being used—ones that have their computer "onboard," inside the robot's body, and others that are linked to a computer via an electronic umbilical cord.

Already, there are many types of robots available, with more to come, and many teachers have begun robotics courses. If you are interested in robots and there are no courses at your school, you might consider talking to one of your teachers. Several teachers might be interested in a course on robotics and might cooperate to set one up. For example, your math teacher might be interested in robots from the point of view of programming and to help teach different areas of math. Your science teacher might be interested in robots as a way to illustrate the new developments in computer science, artificial intelligence, microelectronics, and physics. Your social studies teacher might be able to incorporate robots into his or her discussion about the impact of computers, robots, and automation on society. Your shop teachers might want to play a direct part in a class on building a robot. Many of the skills taught in shop, including draftsmanship, metalworking, carpentry, and electronics, can all be brought together into a course on building a robot.

9

ROBOTS IN
THE HOME

In the late 1970's a robot billed as the "ultimate home appliance" made a tour around the United States. Newspapers and magazines reported that the robot was a marvel of modern technology, capable of taking over a family's housekeeping and cooking chores.

Fortunately, two Carnegie-Mellon University graduate students were suspicious of the claims about the robot. They investigated and, sure enough, found that the robots' promoters—and some gullible members of the news media —had greatly overstated the truth. Left on its own, the robot would have been less competent—or safe—around the house than a housekeeping chimpanzee.

The incident was not unusual. In fact, it was part of a long tradition. Over the ages, people have wanted to believe that a scientist—or wise man—was capable of bringing inanimate matter to life and then able to instruct the creature to take over the menial tasks around the home.

In actuality, there are no real "ultimate household appliance" robots yet in existence. The reason for this is that most people's homes are simply too complicated an environment for a robot. When a robot is used in a factory, everything related to the robot's activities is organized and planned, down to the last detail. This is because robots have limited intelligence and sensory mechanisms. When things are out of place, there is little they can do except cry for help.

Now think of the way things are around your home. Unless your home is very unusual, things probably change all the time. Schedules vary—with people coming and going at different times; things get put in different places or lost; the furniture gets rearranged. Homes are, in fact, enormously complex places. This is why, according to a robotics expert in Washington, D.C., to build an all-purpose, intelligent household robot, "you'd have to build a robot that is a hundred times more complicated than today's industrial robots."

On the other hand, now, more than ever, families could really use a mechanical household helper. Millions of women have left the home and work in jobs alongside the men. Young people are involved in school and after-school activities. Who is going to stay at home, do the laundry, keep the house spick-and-span, and cook good, nutritious meals for the family?

Not too many years ago, when a family needed a domestic servant, they would hire a human being. Nowadays this is done less and less often. Rates for household work have risen sharply, and attitudes have changed. Many people see housework as demeaning. There are few people who will take on the tedious job of cleaning another family's home and cooking their meals. Under these circumstances, a good robot cook and housekeeper would be very much in demand. Unfortunately, such a robot would be far too expensive for the average family budget. As one expert put it, "Who wants to pay $50,000 to get the kitchen sink cleaned?"

THE OUTLOOK FOR HOUSEHOLD ROBOTS

A true, all-purpose housekeeping robot may be a long way off, but robotics is a young science. Many serious inventors —scientists, engineers, and hobbyists—have already begun working toward that distant goal.

How long until we see a household robot that does everything? According to Hans Moravec, a scientist at the Robotics Institute in Pittsburgh, Pennsylvania, it may take around ten or twenty years. Moravec says the first thing we might see is "a robot arm attached to the stove, stirring pots. But we'll quickly move to mobile robots that can open the refrigerator, stir a pot, and put the whole dinner in the microwave."

Working robots have already appeared on television, demonstrating rudimentary skills in housekeeping, but accurately reflecting the current level of robot technology.

For example, a small, new Unimate 250 robot arm recently appeared on TV, set up in front of a curtained window. The robot arm bent over, pulled the curtain cord and opened the curtain. Next it grabbed a window cleaner, sponged the lower pane, flipped the tool over to the rubber-blade side, and proceeded to squeegee the window until it was dry.

But the robot still wasn't finished. It put away the window cleaner, unfastened the window latch, and raised the window. Then, to the delight of the TV audience, it picked up a watering pail and watered the flowers in a box outside the window.

Robot arms and small mobile robots have been used independently. But how about a robot arm mounted on a mobile robot's body? Taking two robots from two different manufacturers and linking them together to form a larger, more versatile robot may be a trend in both industrial and hobby robotics—using smaller, independent, semi-intelligent robots as the building blocks for constructing larger, more complex robots.

It reminds one of the evolution of life forms on our planet. Since we are just getting to the point where robots are able to mimic certain functions of lower animals, it is clear why current robots aren't ready to cope with the knotty, frustrating problems humans cope with daily around the home.

THE EARLY HOUSEHOLD ROBOTS

There are, in fact, numerous "robots" that have been built for household (as opposed to industrial or space-exploration) purposes. These robots are usually radio-controlled or have a very limited memory and intelligence. They may be capable of performing one or two tasks, such as pushing an upright vacuum cleaner or mopping the floor, but they *cannot* do everything. Still, they're a start.

The Advanced Robotics Corporation is advertising a robot sentry that confronts burglars and intruders with a fierce "What are you doing here?" And a robot inventor is working on a "watchdog" robot that patrols the house, looking for burglars.

One of the most famous household robots is Arok, built by Ben Skora (try spelling "Skora" backward). Arok is Ben's latest creation. He is a domestic *android,* a robot that resembles a human being.

Arok took six years to build, at a cost of around $57,000. His onboard computer can be programmed for daily tasks such as walking the dog, serving drinks, or taking out the trash. Needless to say, for Arok to perform each task smoothly, Skora needs to plan everything carefully. Although Arok has touch sensors to keep him from "steamrolling" over household furniture—and people's feet—he works best when there are no obstacles in his path and when household items are exactly where he expects to find them. Although Ben has taken every precaution to make Arok a gentle, safe robot, what happens, one wonders, when the 6-foot-8-inch, 275-pound robot comes whisking along at 3 miles per hour and trips over a baton or broom left carelessly on the floor?

This brings up the whole question of consumer awareness. In the next few years, we may see a flood of new household robots on the market. Comparisons between them will need to be made, since it is very likely that many will do far less than their manufacturer claims, and some will be hazardous and unsafe, especially around small children, pets, and elderly or handicapped people.

FROM HOUSEHOLD SERVANT
TO HOUSEHOLD ASSISTANT

Much of AI research focuses on the development of "smart" robots that help people perform tasks more easily, quickly, and efficiently—in other words, on *intelligent assistants* rather than mechanical household servants. The key here is that people are still doing the job, but the robot is helping them in ways that it can. This approach is attractive, because it enables us to sidestep all the applications like cooking, laundry, dusting, and vacuuming, where robots' skills are still weak, and instead concentrate on areas where robots excel such as in *information processing* and *communication*.

One robot inventor with ideas along these lines is Ken Davis of Phoenix, Arizona. A few years ago, Ken built a 4-foot-10-inch, 205-pound, bullet-shaped robot named Reggie I. Reggie I looks much like R2D2's older brother and spends most of his time entertaining guests at plant openings, electronics shows, and birthday parties.

Davis is now at work on successors to Reggie I—i.e., Reggie II, Reggie III, and Reggie IV. The new models, according to Davis, will not be stage performers like Reggie I, but are going to be employed around the home. What makes Davis's robots seem more practical than other household robots is that they are not intended for housekeeping. Davis's robots will not vacuum or cook. For example, when a newspaper interviewer asked Reggie if he did housework, he replied, "I don't do windows."

Instead, Davis sees his robots as the next step in the evolution of a family's home computer. He looks at them as mobile, intelligent computers with radio links to other household appliances and to the outside world through the telephone, radio receiver, and TV.

Some future version of the robot might tag along with you as you go through the house and act like a mechanical version of Robinson Crusoe's man Friday. You could dictate messages to it, and it would record them and remind you about them later, like an electronic note pad or bulletin board. Or, if you were taking a bath, you could instruct the robot to turn on the record player in the other room—which it would instantly do by sending a radio message. Or, you could have the robot make a phone call, using a radio phone installed on its body. Or, if you needed some information, you could just ask the robot. It would radio the home computer and search the family data base or make a radio phone call and search for the information among any of dozens of electronic libraries.

All of these functions are now possible using today's technology. This is because the goal for these robots is to help us to store, retrieve, and communicate information, and to operate other household appliances by *radio telemetry*. The robots are not expected to perform the far more difficult tasks associated with housework, which require further advances in artificial intelligence, machine vision, machine locomotion, even machine construction.

IF IT MOVES IN, I MOVE OUT!

In today's homes we are deluged with mechanical automata of all types—dishwashers, vacuum cleaners, coffee makers, microwave ovens, computerized chess players. Recently, stories have been published about homeowners who suffer from "high-tech anxiety," a condition in which they feel overwhelmed by all the new, fancy household gadgets and machines. Instead of seeing these machines as wonderful labor-saving devices, they fear them because they are too complicated to operate and repair, and because they feel that, with machines all around them, they are servants to the machines, rather than the other way around.

In fact, robots and other computer-controlled devices are at the crest of a tidal wave of new high-technology household products. How are people reacting to these products?

On one hand, there are news reports about people "murdering" computers—axing them, stabbing them, and smashing them. On the other hand, there are the perennial optimists, whose bubbling enthusiasm for new computerized appliances clouds their common sense.

AN ANSWER FOR THE NEAR FUTURE: ROBOT PETS

One possible way to ease the way for the robot into the average home is as a "pet." The robot, packaged as a cute teddy bear or turtle, instead of a threatening six-footer, could come bumbling and beeping into the home and, shortly thereafter, capture the family's affections.

Why might robot pets be acceptable where robot servants are not? First of all, they are less threatening—maybe not to the dog or cat, but at least to humans. Also, they don't have to do anything complicated or important except be loyal, amusing, and friendly. And they can provide the illusion of real human companionship through conversational programming and computer voice synthesis. Lastly, they can be educational as well as entertaining. They can keep you on your toes with a stimulating stream of word and logic games, spelling, history and number games, and so on.

In the next few years toy robot "pets" will grow rapidly in

popularity and sophistication. Walking, talking, singing, teaching robots are already on the drawing boards of the major electronic toy manufacturers. These products, no doubt, will do a lot to smooth the way for more serious household robots.

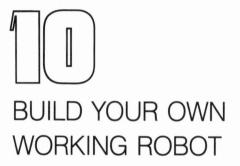

BUILD YOUR OWN
WORKING ROBOT

Do you have to sit still and wait for the robot toys to "grow up" into serious, competent household servants? You could, but that will probably take several years. In the meantime, you might consider joining thousands of other young people around the world who are building robot "assistants" and robot "pets" of their own.

WHAT KIND OF PEOPLE BUILD ROBOTS?

Robot builders seem to be fascinated with machines and with the idea of creating artificial life. True, the motors and gears, the tiny integrated circuits that make up most robots are inert, inorganic materials, but they can now be molded into a machine—a creature, a device, a being—that appears to be at least somewhat intelligent and therefore alive. And there is a strongly felt notion among roboticists that, eventually, machines will become so advanced and their thinking and understanding so complex that we will have to admit that they not only convey the *illusion* of life, but that they are actually alive.

Another characteristic of robot builders is that almost all are tinkerers, people who enjoy putting things together and taking them apart. In fact, this is usually how they get into building a robot. They don't begin by planning out the whole project and by spending years and years preparing themselves—they just stumble into it and start putting things together, one step at a time. This approach may not be the best, but for many people, building a robot is just a natural outgrowth of their interest in machines and their desire to do some tinkering.

Other characteristics of robot builders are their belief in the worth of robotics, their belief that artificial intelligence—and life—can be created. Raj Reddy is the director of the Robotics Institute at Carnegie-Mellon University, in Pittsburgh, Pennsylvania, and one of the foremost researchers in artificial intelligence. According to Reddy, "If you have faith in robots and AI, if you are not afraid of taking risks, and if you dare to do what no one else has done, then you are perfect for this sort of field."

A final major characteristic of people who build their own robots is that they are natural *programmers*. What is a "natural programmer?" It is a person who can look at the big picture, think imaginatively and intuitively, but who also is extremely patient and interested in the nitty-gritty details of what makes something work—in the algorithms, procedures, or schematics that make up robots' hardware and software. The best programmers are people who like to solve puzzles, who are detail-oriented and well organized—people who hate to leave loose ends dangling.

It is exciting the way programs run through a robot's brain at a rate of several thousand instructions a second—almost miraculous the way they bring the robot to life and give it at least the illusion of real intelligence. But programs can be finicky, tedious, enormous recipes that take long hours to prepare and even longer hours to debug if something goes wrong.

Both sides of programming are equally valid—the excitement of watching them run and the drudgery of writing hundreds of lines of detailed commands. One thing is clear, though: Robot builders thrive on both the good and bad in programming. They have the persistence to nurse along a perverse, bug-ridden program until the computer accepts it. Then they can feel the thrill of watching their program "take off" and bring the robot to life.

WHAT TYPE OF ROBOT CAN YOU BUILD?

If you are interested in building a robot by yourself, or with some friends or classmates at school, you need to ask yourself: What kind of robot can I build? What sort of robot do I want to build? These two issues—"can" and "want"—are important for you to consider before you take another step.

First, what kind of robot *can* you build? Many young people decide that they want to build a robot that is just like the robot on TV or in a movie they saw. They acquire some cylindrical cans, some electric motors, some tricycle tires, maybe some accordion-style dryer hose, some lead pipes, and they're ready. Or are they?

The truth is that building a real working robot is serious business. Even so, *no* robot is as smart or sophisticated as the superstar entertainer robots that populate the movie and TV worlds of science fiction. Thousands of engineers, scientists, inventors, and hobbyists are trying to build better robots. But intelligent, humanlike androids are still a long way off. So any young person who wants to build a carbon copy of the *Star Wars* robots, C3PO and R2D2, is headed for disappointment.

Also, remember that you are not some medieval alchemist who can concoct a real working robot out of a few parts you've gathered after an afternoon of scavenging at a local auto body shop. In fact, perhaps the best place to try to build a true working robot is not at home at all. It is at school, where you have resources such as a woodworking shop, a metalworking shop, an electronics shop, drafting equipment, the tools and parts needed to construct the robot, and especially teachers and classmates to give you guidance and encouragement.

On the other hand, there are still very few schools that offer courses in robotics. So what should you do—give up? Never! Instead, why not take it as a challenge? Try to interest your teachers in a course on robotics. If you don't succeed, you *can* build your own working robot at home. You just need to know what you are getting into—*before* you start, not after.

Perhaps the biggest thrill of building a robot by yourself is that you'll be a pioneer, one of the first people in the world to build his own robot. As I've mentioned before, robotics is a young science, where everyone has the chance to invent something totally new. Right now, a hobbyist robot built in a basement can be just as important as robots being made by scientists and engineers working for universities and large corporations.

But what if you don't feel like the pioneer type? That's fine, too. A robot doesn't have to be the most advanced around to be lots of fun, entertaining, and helpful—to be a good pet or assistant. Also, just trying to build a robot is exciting. And this brings you face to face with the second big question you should ask yourself: What sort of robot do I *want* to build?

To answer that question, you have to ask yourself two other questions: How much time am I willing to spend building my robot? What do I want my robot to do? The simplest working robots that just flash lights and "talk" by using a concealed tape recorder can be constructed in just a couple of weekends. More complicated robots with moving arms or radio control might take a month or two—or even longer—to build.

After you have thought about how much time you want to

spend building your robot, ask yourself the really important question: What do I want my robot to do? The answer to this question depends on whether you want a robot pet or a robot assistant. If you want to build a robot pet, you might want your robot to bark, growl, squeak, talk, play music, or follow spoken commands. You might want it to whiz around the floor, spin in a circle, and, in general, act cute and playful.

If, on the other hand, you want a robot assistant, you might want to make the robot more dignified and program it to have the personality of a scientist or engineer. You might want it to be able to access large quantities of information, either from your home computer or, over the phone, from an electronic library. You might want your robot to act like a calculator, quiz you and help you with your homework, follow you around like a mobile electronic scratch pad and remind you of important things you're supposed to do.

Once you know what you want your robot to do, you can decide what it should look like. How big should it be? Should it be made out of plastic or metal? Should it be shaped like a science-fiction robot, like a human or an animal, or like something straight from your imagination?

How will you make your robot move—with legs, wheels, treads, or what? How can you make your robot avoid obstacles, like tables, chairs, and other people? How can you control your robot—by an onboard computer, by a cable, by radio control? How can you make your robot "see"—by ultrasonics, a video camera, infrared? How can you communicate with the robot—by a keyboard, by giving it voice commands, by a picture screen? What will be the robot's "environment"—its familiar surroundings, the place where it will be programmed to operate—inside, outside, or only in your bedroom or living room? How do you make your robot have a mind and a character all its own? Should it obey only your voice? Or should it behave unpredictably (much the way real pets do)?

Before you settle on the final details regarding your robot, you should take a look at some of the robots other people have built. You might consult magazine articles, books, and other robot inventors. You'll learn what people have already done, and you'll be sure to get some new ideas for your own robot. (Be sure to look at the sources at the end of this book.)

HOMEMADE ROBOT EXPLORERS AND ENTERTAINERS

Many young people are building robots that don't fall easily into the category of either "pet" or "assistant." Robert Profeta, of Vineland, New Jersey, inspired by articles he read on the "Mars Rover" robot, built a simple, remote-controlled "explorer" device called SB-3400. Robert made SB-3400 out of materials he could locate cheaply and easily: a motorcycle battery and small DC motors for power, a plastic globe for a head, and plywood for SB-3400's body. Like his NASA counterparts, SB-3400 can measure the temperature of his environment and search for organic matter in a liquid. Robert operates SB-3400 by a hand-held control box and a long cord.

Garner Holt, of San Bernardino, California, is another builder of unusual robotlike devices. Garner's inspiration was "Abraham Lincoln" the animatron—an advanced humanlike automaton that entertains visitors to Disneyland near Los Angeles, California. After seeing the Lincoln automaton, Garner returned to his home and built an automated haunted house in his backyard. Skulls jabbered, birds flew, and his friends loved it.

For the Bicentennial, Garner built a talking head—Uncle Sam. Sam talks and moves his head in twenty-eight lifelike ways. Garner likes to call his creatures "animated figures" instead of robots, since to him robots sound like clanking metallic monsters from outer space. In fact, Garner's inventions are sophisticated automata; they have no intelligence or ability to receive information from the outside world. Once turned on, they always perform the same sequence of movements.

SPECIAL-PURPOSE WORKING ROBOTS

One reason industrial robots are so popular is because they are taking over factory jobs that are too hazardous or boring for human beings. As a robot builder, you could make a great contribution by thinking of places where humans now work —outside the factory, for example—where it might be safer to use a robot.

One roboticist with this philosophy is sixteen-year-old Louis Steinberg of New York City, who wants to build a robot that can run up and down tracks mounted on huge advertising billboards. Presently, people have to be raised and lowered on scaffolds to search for and replace burned-out bulbs from among the billboards' hundreds of tiny lights. Louis' robots could swiftly run up and down the tracks and replace the bulbs under the remote control of a human operator located safely on the ground.

Another robot that might be combined with Louis' billboard robots is a robot named Herb designed by Holden Caine, an eighteen-year-old student at the Rochester Institute of Technology. Herb (which stands for Holden's Electronic Roving Brain) has one major goal: to find and approach the brightest light. Herb is computer-controlled and, like the tiny robot mice, can negotiate his way through a maze of obstacles separating him from the bright light his programming tells him to approach.

You might consider designing a counterpart to Herb that would look for the darkest spot in a room rather than the brightest spot. This might be the first step to designing a special-purpose robot assistant that could race up and down a billboard, searching for and replacing burned-out bulbs.

GETTING STARTED: ARTICLES, BOOKS, AND CATALOGS

You have decided you really want to build your own robot. The question is: How do you get started?

There are several ways to take your first step: (1) you can read some of the many "how-to" books and articles; (2) you can send away for catalogs from electronics and robot-parts supply stores; (3) you can buy one of the many robot kits that are appearing on the market; (4) if you have a home computer, you can learn a lot about robots and artificial intelligence by simulating a robot on your computer.

FIRST LEARN THE BASICS

How do you go from building a simple robot to constructing a more sophisticated one? Let's assume you are just getting started. In that case, you need to do two things: *Find out about all the parts that go into a robot, and learn how a relatively sophisticated robot is assembled.*

One way to get an overview of a robot's parts, or components, is to take a look at books on robotics. Familiarize yourself with potentiometers, DC motors, the various types of batteries, phototransistors, and strain gauges. Then read about some of the options you have regarding power sources, wiring and electronics-circuit diagrams, sensors, types of computer control, radio control, and so on. Check out one or two books on "principles of electricity" and "principles of electronics." You should also learn about digital circuits, metalworking, carpentry, drafting, and design.

Then work with several "electronics project" kits from an electronics store. These kits will give you experience at working with simple electronics circuits. They will help teach you some basic skills such as soldering, wire-wrapping, and troubleshooting for defective components (chips, resistors, diodes, transistors, et cetera) or for errors you have made, either in designing your project or in putting it together.

SIMULATING A ROBOT ON A COMPUTER

If your family—or school—has a computer, the next step you might want to take is to simulate a robot using the computer. This is an inexpensive, fascinating way for you to learn what types of functions you'll want for your robot and how you might go about implementing those functions.

What is *robot simulation*? Usually it means: (1) constructing a two-dimensional image of a robot and its environment on the computer's picture screen; (2) creating a set of "robot commands" that, when typed into the computer, will cause your picture-screen robot to interact with its environment.

The robot in a simulation can be a simple square "blip" on the screen or an elaborate robot with wheels and arms, all in full color. The "environment" can be an image of a table with blocks, a chessboard, a floor full of obstacles, a maze, or whatever.

Robot simulation is a tool that is used quite often in industry as well as in laboratory research and development. Researchers can thoroughly test and debug programs on a simulated robot and on a variety of simulated work stations before transferring the programs to a real robot working at a real work station. This approach will save the researchers time, money, and probably quite a few headaches.

Another reason to simulate robots on a computer screen is to avoid building a real mechanical robot. Many people are more intrigued with the "idea" of a robot and of what a robot might do than they are with trying to build a real robot. *Microbots*—robot images on microcomputer television displays—allow you to focus on issues related to real working robots without having to build one.

One of the most exciting things about Microbots is that they are also useful in teaching you about computer graphics (or picture making), an important part of any computer adventure game or sports game. Learning how to create a sophisticated Microbot will give you many of the techniques you'll need to create animated screen displays and intelligent, unpredictable monsters and players for your own favorite video game. Sophisticated Microbots can become clever, unpredictable players, heroes, and monsters in your video games. Likewise, a complex Microbot room, or environment, can be converted into an electronic game board, soccer field, or enchanted forest.*

CONVERTING TOYS AND KITS INTO WORKING ROBOTS

If you still don't feel ready to build a real working robot from scratch, you might first try converting a toy into a robot or building a robot from a kit.

The value of working with a toy robot is that you won't have to do much physical construction, and the toy robots are usually relatively inexpensive. One toy you might want to experiment with is Big Trak by Milton Bradley, which already has an onboard computer (a Texas Instruments TMS 1000, 4-bit microcomputer). Big Trak on its own can execute up to thirty program steps (with the RPT, or "repeat," command), and it can go up to 99 feet in a single direction on only a single command. But this is only the start if you are willing to modify the toy and link it to an external "mother" computer.

With some ingenuity and experimentation, you can convert a relatively inexpensive toy like Big Trak into a working robot that interacts with its environment and can operate under

*Some new computer games enable you to program your own Microbots (picture-screen robots), for example, Robotwar from MUSE Software, 330 North Charles Street, Baltimore, MD 21201.

computer control. Wireless control (allowing the computer to transmit commands and receive information from Big Trak up to 200 feet) is quite advanced, since a relatively powerful home computer becomes the robot's brain. This means that the robot can have quite a high degree of programmed intelligence and interact with its environment in a rather sophisticated manner. These are nice features, given the low cost of the robot and the basically simple hardware modifications required.

Another way to build a working robot is to buy a robot kit. Kits are a good way to start for at least three reasons: (1) the kit comes to you already half built; (2) it comes with all the parts you're supposed to need; and (3) the (good) kit comes with detailed instructions on how to put all the parts together.

Many good kits are already out on the market. You can read about them in hobbyist magazines and hobby robot catalogs. Two of the older, tested kits you might consider are

THE TURTLE ROBOT From Terrapin, Inc., Cambridge, Massachusetts

The Turtle is operated, via a cable, by programs running on your home or classroom computer. It can be programmed to roll around, beep, blink its two LED "eyes," sense contact with another object, and draw rough pictures and geometric figures using the ball-point pen fastened to its belly.

THE ET-2 SHELL From Lour Control, Schaumberger, Illinois

This is a basic unit to which you have to add your own power source and (computer) control circuits. The 2-foot-high, 14-inch-wide robot *shell* comes with two independently driven wheels and four bumper switches that enable the robot to sense when it runs into another object. Additional features, such as a manipulator (arm) and an ultrasonic detector, are being planned for the ET-2.

"BUILD-IT-YOURSELF" ROBOT BOOKS

After you have built a robot from a kit, you are probably ready to tackle one of the build-it-from-scratch robot books.

"How-to" books can be helpful in many ways: (1) the parts the books recommend are relatively cheap; (2) you can gradually make the robot more complex—you don't have to do it all at once; and (3) the "how-to" books guide you through all the mechanical (hardware) and programming (software) details related to the robot's construction. This attention to detail and clarity keeps the beginner from wandering off the track and getting lost and frustrated. (Several how-to books are listed at the back of this book.)

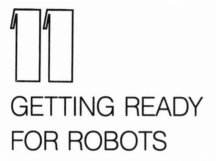

GETTING READY
FOR ROBOTS

There are several reasons for studying robotics. Robots and their related technologies promise to have a huge impact on our economy and society. It will be easier for you to make important future decisions if you have some knowledge of these technologies and can assess their influence on your life.

Also, by actually building a robot in a course, you will pick up a lot of important knowledge in a number of fields, such as electronics, computer programming, mechanical, electrical and industrial engineering, with emphasis on automation as a method of solving problems and accomplishing a task.

You will also acquire a number of valuable skills, including an ability to work as part of a team that designs and builds a finished product; and skills in communications (reading, writing, speaking, and listening), problem-solving, planning, and record keeping. Furthermore, building a robot will sharpen your math.

Another reason to study robots is that robotics offers many

career opportunities, since it is a focal point for some of the most pervasive new technologies being developed in our society, such as microelectronics, computers, and artificial intelligence.

The worldwide electronics industry, for example, is a $100-billion-a-year industry now and likely to grow to $800 billion by the late 1980's. Products from this industry—computers, robots, games, and other devices—are already beginning to flood our schools, our homes, our offices and factories. They seem destined to change significantly the way we work and play.

One result of these technologies will be to displace massive numbers of workers—in factories, in offices, in retail, banking, insurance, and other industries susceptible to automation, even in the electronics industry itself.

On the other hand, the microelectronics and robotics "revolutions" *will* generate a great many new jobs. Specialists will be sought after in computers, robotics, artificial intelligence, computer vision and computer speech, microcircuits, and in automation itself. Whether you wish to work in private industry, in government, or as an independent consultant, you will find there is a great demand for people in each of these areas.

Schools and other educational institutions in our society must greatly enlarge their curricula in the areas of robotics, computers, and microelectronics in order for young people to be sufficiently aware of forthcoming social and economic changes and to land jobs when they leave school.

Experts foresee a growing need for people who can repair and maintain robots, but there are few schools that offer programs in this area, since getting a classroom industrial robot for students to work on is too expensive.

Fortunately, this situation is changing rapidly. Companies are starting their own training institutes, and robot manufacturers are discounting and donating industrial robots to new programs being set up by colleges, universities, and vocational

training schools. Also, students can acquire many of the
necessary skills by building robots that are significantly cheaper
than those used in industry.

ROBOTICS COURSES

Pioneering courses in robot technologies are springing up
around the country—in high schools, in technical schools, and
in colleges and universities. The most widespread programs in
robotics today, however, are run by robot manufacturers and
the major industrial users of robots.

Opinions are mixed as to the present and projected needs for
different types of jobs in robotics. Many experts agree with Dr.
Raj Reddy, director of Carnegie-Mellon's Robotics Institute,
that there is not *currently* a big demand for mechanics to repair
disabled robots. The robots are constructed in easily replace-
able modules, they rarely break down, and there are still too
few robots installed to justify someone's becoming an expert in
robot repair alone. Some experts also feel that most major
robot users will train their own people.

On the other hand, there may be a demand in the future for
maintenance personnel. A typical company will employ robots
around the clock—three shifts a day. To keep the robots
running, the company will also need three shifts of hardware
and software maintenance personnel to service them.

Also, United States robot manufacturers and the United
States government are becoming alarmed over the growing
success of Japanese manufacturers in selling robots in this
country. Some observers predict that, by the late 1980's,
Japanese manufacturers may capture as much as 40 percent of
the United States robot market, which has been growing at
about 50 percent per year. At this pace, in 1990, two billion
dollars' worth of robots will be sold to domestic manufacturers
and other customers. United States robot producers are determined not to lose this enormous market to the Japanese. They

are building new, automated robot-producing factories and hiring thousands of new employees.

Most expert observers feel that, over the next twenty years, the world robotics industry might grow as large as the world automobile industry. The first robots were the big, hefty types employed in heavy industry. But thousands of new, smaller robots are being developed and will find jobs in all sectors of our economy—offices, schools, homes, small industry, retail businesses, banks, and so on. As robots proliferate, manufacturers alone will not be able to train adequate numbers of people to install the robots, repair them, and maintain them.

Already, manufacturers are becoming aware of this projected shortage, and they are donating and discounting robots to schools both in Europe and the United States. In this way, students can receive training on many kinds of machines and can learn how to install, program, repair, and maintain a great variety of computers, robots, and other forms of automated equipment.

TRAINING FOR THE FUTURE
IN CAD/CAM, CAMIS AND VHSIC

Robots are only the tip of a gigantic iceberg of new systems and technologies that will contribute to the automation of our factories and offices. Robots will actually perform the work, but they will only be the pawns in large complicated systems controlled by computers and monitored by humans.

Factories of the future will be automated through CAD CAM, which stands for Computer-Aided Design/Computer-Aided Manufacturing. The United States government and major corporations and universities are investing millions of dollars in efforts to integrate and automate all functions in companies that design and manufacture products, from those associated with our defense needs to goods we use every day. All may soon be designed cheaper and better with CAD/CAM.

A technology that will influence all sectors of modern society is the Computer-Aided Makeup and Imaging System (CAMIS). CAMIS is one of the routes to the paperless society, a society in which computer terminals replace everything from telephone directories to books, accounting ledgers, and business memos.

A third technology is the Electronic Funds Transfer System (EFTS). Banks and other financial institutions are working to install EFTS in order to convert the massive amount of checks and cash flowing through our society into electronic money, zipping about, via communications satellite, from one computer to another.

And lastly, there is the technology of Very High-Speed Integrated Circuits (VHSIC). The U.S. Air Force has been sponsoring a $10-million-dollar effort to develop this new generation of super-small, super-fast microchip brains and memories that will significantly change the whole field of computers and computer programming. The chips will be so small, so powerful, and so cheap that they will be able to incorporate—right in their tiny circuits—many of the programs now being written by computer programmers.

All these technologies—robots, CAD/CAM, CAMIS, EFTS, and VHSIC—are going to work together and have a huge impact on our economy's "information sector." Already more than half of our nation's gross national product is derived from the information sector. According to *Computer Career News*, "widespread computerization of that economic segment will bring new demands to an already short labor market for computer specialists while eliminating many less technical jobs."

The U.S. Department of Labor echoes this prediction. The latest department statistics show that jobs for computer professionals will increase nearly 84 percent by 1990, more than four times the projected growth rate for all other occupations in the country.

Spurred on by several supporting technologies, robots and smart computers will soon be penetrating all areas of our economy. At the same time that they are causing sizable displacements in the blue- and white-collar labor force, they will be generating many new jobs. These new jobs—in robotics, artificial intelligence, computer programming, computer servicing, systems analysis, electrical and mechanical engineering, automation, production control—will be considerably more complicated and specialized than in the past. To qualify for these jobs people will need special training. If predictions are accurate, before long all unskilled, low-level clerical, supervisory, and factory jobs will simply disappear.

Where can you get the necessary training to design, install, program, and maintain robots and smart computers? Where can you learn to develop the hardware and software required for CAD/CAM, CAMIS, VHSIC, and EFT systems? A good place to start is in high school or a vocational-technical school. Later you can continue your studies at the university level and at government- and company-sponsored training centers. Many state governments are also beginning to recognize the enormous economic potential of the electronics-based industries and are imitating the successful Japanese model by encouraging cooperation among local government, local universities, and locally based corporations to try to attract more industry to the state.

Finally, there are quite a few institutes and centers being established by private firms and government agencies. Many of these organizations will soon be giving young people on-the-job training in conjunction with their work at a local college, technical school, or university. (For the names and addresses of robotic training centers, be sure to look at "Materials and Schools" at the back of this book.)

THE WORKING ROBOT:
SERVANT, FRIEND, OR FOE?

A consensus is growing among robot and computer experts that we are on the brink of a new era in which robots and intelligent computers will play an enormous part in our lives. Robots in the factories will soon become more sophisticated and spawn robots in the office, robots on the farm, robots in the classroom, and robots in the home. New generations of young people will have to master new skills and attitudes in order to manage, repair, maintain, and improve these robots.

Many people now working will lose their jobs to robots. Some will become permanently unemployed and probably will become extremely bitter toward robots. Others will be unable to make the leap to a new job or career. They, too, will blame the robots for their troubles. Still others will be immediately relocated and retrained, it is hoped in a more satisfying, more rewarding field.

The United States is in a difficult position. During the last few decades, productivity has dropped off and the economy has stagnated. Other countries have faced similar problems, but now they are quickly moving ahead, investing heavily in microelectronics, computers, and robots. These appear to be profitable "growth" industries, and their increased use will make a country's economy vastly more productive and competitive.

Essentially, we are all in a gigantic race. We are all scrambling to "reindustrialize" our countries. That means we must tear apart all our old factories, stores, and offices, and then start from scratch, making sure we have plenty of computers, electronics, and robots this next time around. The country that finishes rebuilding its economy first—and best—will have a tremendous competitive and economic edge over all the other countries of the world.

All of this is just to explain why, in America and elsewhere, companies are rushing to install robots and new computers; why the "automated factory" and the "paperless office" are swiftly becoming realities, backed by huge funding from large corporations and from the federal government.

Because of this rush to automate and increase productivity, there is no question that people are going to be displaced by machines—by robots and smart computers. The real questions, then, are: How soon? How many people? Can and will they be retrained? How about you and other young people? In an automated, "robotized" economy, what careers will you find? Which ones are satisfying? Which are secure?

ROBOTS THAT PLAN, LEARN, AND HAVE GOALS

Most robots presently on the job have no knowledge of the outside world. All they have is a sequence of instructions that they obey, causing them to move their arms and hands from one position to another. Newer robots will be quite different. They will come with a "world model," a data bank of information stored in their computer brain. They will have information about the factory, about their tasks, and about themselves. This information is a primitive version of the experience and knowledge a human factory worker has stored inside his or her memory.

With the new information, the robot will no longer blindly execute instructions. Instead, it will be programmed to have a goal. Equipped with vision and perhaps tactile sensors, it will be able to plan how to perform various tasks and will "learn" from its experience each time it does so.

The next step will be to link together "discretionary" or decision-making robots and have them all report to a computer "foreman." As the robots work, they will be on the lookout for problems. If, for example, they notice an unusual number of defects in parts they are welding or assembling, they will notify the foreman to take corrective action.

When independent teams of robots become available, it won't be long until the arrival of the automated, or unmanned, factory. In the United States a project known as Integrated Computer-Aided Manufacturing (ICAM) is under way. The U.S. Air Force is investing $16 million dollars a year to develop factories that will have computer tools and robot operations; computer management of inventory, parts, and work flow; computer design of parts; and a "boss" computer programming the operation of all the worker robots and computers in the factory.

What will evolve as part of the new automated factories is a new robot, what James Albus has called a *controller* or *distributed intelligence,* similar to the computer Hal in the movie *2001.* These "super robots" will have perhaps dozens of individual, stand-alone robots for their arms and legs, their eyes and ears. And they will be in command of a hierarchy of microcomputers, which will do all the detailed work for them. The new factory controller-robots will spend their time coordinating the entire factory, keeping it on schedule, and monitoring and responding to special emergencies. They won't be stand-alone robots that you can walk up to and see. Instead, they'll be everywhere, but invisible. All the robots you see working will be like the eyes, the ears, and the limbs of a super robot that will occupy an entire factory. In fact, the factory itself will be the robot.

INDIVIDUALIZED AUTOMATION

Michael Dertouzos, a scientist at MIT, carries the robot factory another step further. He proposes that once these factories become possible (within the next ten to twenty years), they should be miniaturized and located in the commercial district in cities and towns. Then customers who needed a new, customized product could order it and have it created for them while they waited in the store.

Take shoes, for example. The less expensive and the more personalized they are, the better. In the near future, small, robot shoe factories might be built right behind downtown shoe stores. Customers will come in and choose the style of shoe they want from a huge catalog of shoe styles. Or they may design their own. Imagine the following scene:

After choosing a shoe, the customer sits down on a robot that automatically sizes his or her foot. The robot hands the customer a magnetic card with the correct size noted for future visits to the shoe store. The robot feeds a second copy of the card into the main computer, which instructs an automatic cutting table to cut the pattern for the shoes out of a raw material such as leather. Then a team of robots constructs the shoe. Only minutes after the customer has placed the order, the new shoes pop through the door and are ready to be put on. The shoes fit well, they are cheap, and they are exactly what the customer desired.

THE GREAT DEBATE: PEOPLE'S JOBS VERSUS ROBOTS' PRODUCTIVITY

"Individualized automation" sounds very desirable, but we must think about its impact on the economy and the society at large. For example, imagine robots taking over the production of goods and services in mini-factories located in cities and towns all over the country. What's the result? Chances are we'll have more shoes, clothes, tools, appliances, and other consumer and industrial products than we'll know what to do with. "Productivity" is the robots' middle name—they're experts at it.

In an automated, "robotized" economy, the robots will be the producers, since they're the best at producing. But what will the rest of us be doing?

James Albus, a scientist at the National Bureau of Standards, in Washington, D.C., has spent a lot of time trying to answer that question. Albus is one of the few people bold enough to look forward far enough to the social and economic consequences of the second industrial revolution—the robotics revolution.

We already have abundant predictions about the number of robots that will soon be welding, inspecting parts, performing batch assembly, and palletizing. What we do not hear about is what happens when huge numbers of robots move into the factories and offices. Surely this will mean a great change in the way our economy runs, but what kind of change? How should we be preparing for this change? According to Albus,

> In a robotic society we won't work. The robots will do most jobs more efficiently than we could do them. Such robots can usher in an age of superabundant, very inexpensive goods. But there's a hitch. If humans don't work, do they deserve to be paid? Where can they get the money to buy all the wonderful and inexpensive products the robots will produce?

> We can't have a society of unemployed people who can't afford the products made for them by the robots that took away their jobs. That's absurd. We must devise a scheme that will shift the manner in which we receive income without endangering either our standard of living or our self-respect.

Albus calls his scheme "people's capitalism," and it carries individualized automation another step further. Albus foresees a future when robotic factories will make huge quantities of manufactured goods that cost little more than the raw materials that went into them. The problem will be how to distribute the wealth generated by the goods and services pouring from an automated economy. Imagine, if you will, he says, robot offices and factories owned by everybody. The wealth of the offices and factories would be distributed to everybody, just as stock dividends are today. The entire population would be secure. Since wages would no longer be the means for distributing wealth, robots would no longer threaten people's basic income. Instead, the robots would generate the income, not endanger it.

Most robotics experts agree with Albus that in time robots will cause a massive displacement of workers in our economy. The real debate centers instead on *when,* not *if.* How quickly will the robots take over factory jobs? How soon can we expect robots in the office? In the store? Working as electronics technicians, appliance repairmen, and servants in our homes?

Joseph Engelberger, the president of Unimation, is the "father of industrial robotics." Engelberger is the primary spokesperson for the gradual robotization of our economy. He admits that there will be disruptions and dislocations, but as he sees it, clerical and blue-collar workers will be turned into what he calls *knowledge workers*—robot programmers, robot designers, electronics specialists, automated-design specialists—all the people needed to support the new technology and keep it running.

Engelberger also points to the humanizing effect of robots in the workplace. Ever since the Industrial Revolution in the late 1700's, people have had to imitate machines in order to perform machinelike jobs, which tend to be repetitious, tedious, boring, and often dangerous. These are just the jobs that robots do best. Now, where robots have been introduced, the worker no longer has to do the machine's job and he or she can supervise and troubleshoot the robots.

Engelberger recommends that people stop looking at robotization as a gigantic tidal wave threatening to engulf our whole society. Instead, he says, look at it at the individual level, factory by factory, office by office, job by job. This way you can come up with solutions that are fair—for the company, for its employees, and for society at large.

But there are other robotics experts who are strong disbelievers in the technological fix. They see robotization occurring at a much higher rate than Engelberger does. And, if that happens, the workers will be leaving their jobs not through attrition, but through force. It won't be their decision to leave, it will be the company's.

One expert who worries a lot about robotization is Harley Shaiken, a consultant to the United Auto Workers and a Fellow at MIT. Shaiken says he is not an opponent of robots, just an opponent of the harmful ways in which they might be used. They're the ultimate laborsaving device, and saving labor means displacing human workers—at a far greater rate than Engelberger predicts. Shaiken points out that robots are not vulnerable to attrition the way people are and that one robot can take the job of at least three people (by working three shifts—around the clock). He feels that, as early as 1990, robots will take over at least a hundred thousand jobs—just in one industry, the auto industry.

In addition, Shaiken is afraid that, due to efficiency and productivity concerns, management will make human workers speed up to the robots' level, rather than slow the robots down to the level of human beings. Like Engelberger, Shaiken recommends that robots be introduced into the workplace on the basis of attrition. But, unlike Engelberger, he feels that most corporations are already bringing in robots at a much faster rate. Also like Engelberger, Shaiken sees a need for retraining. But, he says, there are thousands of factory workers who are virtually incapable of being retrained. They actually like their particular job, even if it is boring and repetitious. They're good at it, and it's all they've ever done. They don't want to be retrained.

Furthermore, Shaiken says, it's unrealistic to think of jobs just in statistical terms. A computer-programming job may open up in Houston at the same time a robot replaces a human auto worker in Detroit or Dearborn. But it's ridiculous to think that the auto worker is automatically going to move to Houston and become a programmer. The real world doesn't work that way. Instead, there is going to be unemployment and suffering and a huge number of people will be put on welfare.

Engelberger's answer to all this is, again, that robotization will not occur this quickly or harshly. But, even if it does, even if we have to pay a high cost, ultimately it will be worth it. As a society and as an economy, our back is against the wall. Our economy is decaying, productivity is stagnating. Robots are our key to an enormous new level of productivity, which, in the long run, will create jobs, or at least a comfortable standard of living, for all. And unless we move quickly and bring in the robots, someone else will do it—either Japan or Western Europe. And if we allow other countries to jump into the lead, we may never be able to overtake them. Their products will be far cheaper and of a far higher quality than ours. As a result, our economy will wilt. And then we'll find out what *real* unemployment means.

ROBOTS BUILDING ROBOTS

The Unimation plant in Danbury, Connecticut, will soon begin using Unimation robots to build new Unimation robots. Robots will be creating other robots. Many of Japan's robot builders already have robot factories "manned" by other robots. Perhaps the time is not far off when unmanned, automated factories will construct all of our robots. When that time comes, the robots will have another thing in common with human beings: They will be completely self-reproducing.

The Industrial Revolution made "machines" of human beings. It created inhuman work under inhuman conditions, then forced humans to do it. It is possible that we are now in the midst of a second industrial revolution, in which machine-like jobs are returned to machines.

As smart robots master increasingly sophisticated jobs, isn't there a chance of their taking over someday? Will there ever be a robot "uprising," as in Hollywood and science-fiction visions of the future?

Hans Berliner, a computer expert, has a quick solution to a robot uprising: "If intelligent machines make us uncomfortable, we can always pull the plug." Actually, Berliner's solution, though it might make us feel a little better, is not a solution at all. Any machine intelligent enough to pose a real threat to us will also be intelligent enough to prevent us from pulling the plug.

Regardless of the long-term problems of truly intelligent machines, we are already becoming increasingly dependent on smarter and smarter machines—computers and robots of every size, function, and description. And, in a way, doesn't this growing dependence represent a takeover of a sort?

Also, there is a major paradox arising from our development of computer and robot "servants" that are increasingly intelligent and independent. As we increase the intelligence of our machines, we decrease the chances the machines are going to listen to us and do things our way. Independence that improves efficiency is good, since we desperately need better, more efficient ways to solve our problems and run our world. On the other hand, as our robot and computer servants become more intelligent, we lose more and more control over what those servants are doing and how they do it. The question is when, if ever, will machines become too intelligent for their—and our—own good?

FINAL PERSPECTIVES

For millennia, we humans have been creating robots. Heroic or horrible creatures of myth and legend stalk across the ages of humankind and take their place alongside clever automata, the "almost" robots that have delighted and frightened young and old alike.

We have been creating imitation humans—in fact and fantasy—throughout all of recorded history. What is this fascination we humans have for these devices? Perhaps it is our desire to create a modern-day class of slaves. We can bully these new slaves and make them work long, punishing hours doing menial, dangerous, repetitive, inhuman tasks, and *we don't have to feel guilty*. We are not exploiting or degrading either man or beast.

Or, perhaps, the true reason why we are fascinated with robots is that we have, through the ages, become profoundly lonely. We have become painfully aware that we are the only truly intelligent life form on our planet, that we alone shoulder the responsibility for taking care of it. This is an enormous burden. Perhaps the frequent reports of UFOs and of imminent, intelligent robots are symptoms of a yearning we feel to share our extraordinary responsibilities.

Another possible source for our age-old fascination with robots is that we sense in the robots the next step of evolution of intelligent life on this planet. Possibly, we humans are to be the midwives at the birth of a new, advanced life form. In fact, many artificial-intelligence scientists see themselves in precisely this role.

In the past, evolution proceeded along organic, biological lines, but always with mutation—the catalyst for abrupt and radical change—playing a major role. Now these scientists see evolution as again ready to make a giant, startling leap forward, this time in the form of intelligent—even ultra-intelligent—machines. Look around you, the scientists say. We humans are in a terrible mess. We are perched on the twin precipices of nuclear holocaust and ecological disaster. In order to save us from ourselves, we need a true *deus ex machina* (a "god from the machine") in the form of an ultra-intelligent robot or computer.

We human beings are not trying to create something that will replace us. We represent something unique. Even after we have created ultra-intelligent machines, we will still have a special role to play. We and the robots will share many features, but we will still be the best at being human and therefore we'll continue along our own branch on the tree of evolution. Except that there will be a new branch on the tree—*a branch reserved for the robots.*

GLOSSARY

Algorithm The step-by-step plan followed by a robot's computer program to make the robot perform some function, such as "seeing" or playing chess.

Allophone Part of phoneme (word sound). The smallest unit of speech that distinguishes one sound from another. For example, the aspirated *p* of *push* and the nonaspirated *p* of *Spain* represent the two allophones of the phoneme *p*. Allophones can give a robot a more natural-sounding voice than can phonemes.

Analog A continuous electronic signal that exactly reproduces some physical phenomenon outside a computer, such as sound waves, the temperature in a room, et cetera. Since the robot's brain is a digital computer that uses electronic signals at only two levels (either high-low or on-off), it must change any signals from the outside world from analog to digital. And whenever the computer sends signals, it must change its digital signals to analog ones that can, for example, power a hi-fi speaker or give the robot a voice.

Articulations Joints of a robot's arm or leg.

Artificial Intelligence The science of making a machine do things that would require intelligence if done by humans.

Asimov's Laws The "Three Laws of Robotics" created by Isaac Asimov: (1) A robot may not injure a human being, or through inaction allow a human being to come to harm. (2) A robot must obey the orders given it by human beings except where such orders would conflict with the First Law. (3) A robot must protect its own existence as long as such protection does not conflict with the First or Second Law.

Assembly   Picking up parts off a conveyor line and putting them together. New smart, "seeing" robots are beginning to replace humans on the factory assembly line.

Audio-Animatrons   Talking, moving machines pioneered by Walt Disney Productions in their various amusement parks. The machines are not true robots, since they have no way of interacting with the outside world and are preprogrammed to do the same thing over and over again.

Automated Factory   A factory with a smart computer supervising a team of robot workers, where raw materials are converted into finished products with little or no human labor.

Automation   The replacement of human and animal labor by machines.

Automaton   (Pl. *Automata,* pronounced "aw-TOH-mah-tah"). A device that repeats the same function over and over and has little or no interaction with the outside world, for example, a stereo record player or a dishwasher.

Batch Manufacturing   Assembling different parts in a variety of ways to make finished products with individual styles or designs. New, smaller, smarter robots are being "trained" to do batch assembly.

Binary   A robot's computer brain processes and recalls information in the form of two kinds of electronic signals: on-off or high-low. Computer programmers and designers use a zero ("0") to represent an "off" or "low" signal and a one ("1") to represent an "on" or "high" signal. Strings of zeros and ones, in turn, represent coded information: numbers, letters, words and symbols.

Bionics   The field that takes natural processes performed by living creatures and tries to construct machine and artificial likenesses.

Bit (*B*inary dig*IT*).   A one ("1") or zero ("0") in the computer's brain or memory. A bit appears in the form of a pulse or voltage charge of electricity.

Body   Real working robots have bodies in all shapes, colors, and sizes. Their bodies fit the task the robots were built to perform. The robots rarely resemble the humanlike robots of science fiction.

Brain   Human and robot brains both use binary, on-off signals to store and process information. But human and robot brains are physically very different. Robot brains are made of crystalline computers, and human brains of soft, spongy cells. Robot brains do things extremely fast but one thing at a time. Human brains do things relatively slowly but can handle many things at the same time.

Bug   A mistake or error in the program controlling the robot's computer brain. "Bugs" is also used to refer to computer ICs, since they resemble flat, black caterpillars.

Byte   A unit of information formed by stringing eight "bits" (binary digits) together. Depending on the code, a byte might represent a number ("00101101" = "45") or a letter ("01000001" = "A").

CAD/CAM   (Computer-Aided Design/Computer-Aided Manufacturing)   Companies use computerized drafting tables to design new products. Then the characteristics of the product are sent electronically to factory computers and robots that manufacture the product automatically.

CCD (Charge-Coupled Device)   A special type of computer memory chip, ideal for capturing pictures and images. CCDs are being used as electronic, filmless cameras and as "eyes" for robots.

Chip   A square slice of silicon the size of a cornflake and as thin as a human hair. Inlaid on its surface are microcomputer circuits capable of processing a million instructions a second and storing thousands of bits of information. When electricity flows through these circuits, the chip becomes a tiny computing "engine" that remembers or processes information. Also known as *microchip*.

Circuit   A pathway for electricity to flow. Electronic circuits in a robot's computer brain guide and route the flow of information. Typical circuits are transistors, resistors, capacitors, and diodes.

Command   An instruction to the robot's computer given in a language or form the computer can understand.

Computer   A device that accepts, stores, reshapes, and processes information and commands, based on a sequence of instructions (a program) stored in its memory. A computer is so versatile because: (1) it is so fast; (2) it can make decisions; (3) its memory can be erased and new instructions can be fed in at any time. A computer can be used as a "brain" to control any other device or machine, such as a robot.

Computer-Controlled   A robot can be controlled by a tiny microcomputer mounted somewhere on the robot's body. Or the robot can be connected, via radio or a cable, to a minicomputer or home computer.

Continuous-Path Robot   A robot arm that follows the exact path taught to it by its trainer.

Control Program   A program stored permanently in the computer's memory to oversee and coordinate all of the computer's functions.

Coordination   Robots, like people, need to relate their movements to what they see (hand-to-eye coordination), and relate the movements of each limb with all other limbs (hand-to-hand coordination and leg-to-leg coordination).

CPU (*Central Processing Unit*)   A special-purpose chip or a portion of a chip that obeys instructions fed into the computer. The CPU can do arithmetic, make logical decisions, and manipulate words and symbols.

Criminal Robot   Law-enforcement agencies fear an outbreak of robot robberies, arson, sabotage, and terrorism, when the new generation of small, mobile, smart robots appears, sometime in the mid-1980s.

Cybernetics   The science of control—how machines and living creatures control important functions and processes and how they interact with the outside world.

Cyborg   From science fiction: an artificially produced human being. The question is whether a cyborg is a super-sophisticated robot or a human who was created artificially.

Data   Information in the form of bits (ones and zeros) stored and processed by the robot's computer brain in the form of voltage charges and pulses of electricity.

Data Base   Information available to the robot. Similar to a human's memory.

Degrees of Freedom   The different ways a robot's limb (arm or leg) can move—up, down, sideways, rotate, extend, contract, et cetera.

Digital   See *Analog.*

Digitize   When information enters a robot's computer brain, it must be digitized, or converted into ones and zeros representing high-low or on-off electrical charges. See *Analog.*

Distributed Intelligence   The control of bodily functions in a robot does not take place only in the brain. In the future, tiny microcomputers will be placed all over a robot's body to handle different bodily functions (such as walking). In a factory, smart computers and robots will be coordinated by an ultra-intelligent computer "foreman." Yet they will act as "distributed intelligences" that can assemble and manufacture new products on their own.

Drive System   The source of a robot's power. Its motor, power supply, gears, cables, pistons, et cetera.

Drone   A mobile device with a manipulator (or arm). A drone is controlled by a human operator (either riding onboard or guiding the drone by remote control). A drone has little or no ability to make decisions on its own.

Edge Detection   One method a robot (or computer) may use to understand what it "sees." After the robot's camera "eyes" take a picture of an object, the robot tries to recognize the object by finding all the object's edges and comparing the object's outline with objects stored in its memory.

Electronics   The use of electricity to carry information, not just power.

Exoskeleton   A hollow robot shell. A human can climb inside an exoskeleton and operate it by moving his limbs. The device acts as a muscle-amplifier and multiplies the human's normal strength.

Expert System   New computer or robot with an "intelligent" program that gives it Ph.D.-level knowledge and problem-solving abilities. There are expert systems working with humans in biochemistry, geology, medicine, and many other areas.

Feedback   Information received from the outside world regarding some action taken by a robot. A true working robot has sensors that detect the results of its decisions and actions so it can evaluate these results to help it make new decisions and take new actions.

Flyby Robot Probes   Robot spaceships that fly by the sun and by the solar system's other planets and their moons.

Governor   A machine that looks after another machine to make sure it doesn't get out of control. An air-conditioner thermostat is a type of governor. If the air conditioner cools a house below the temperature chosen by one of the occupants of the house, the thermostat "notices" this and cuts the power to the air conditioner.

Gray Scale   The brightness of each part of an object. A computer "sees" an object as a tile mosaic made up of hundreds of thousands of little "tiles" of light or darkness. Each tile (or "pixel"—picture cell) is stored in the computer's memory either as "white" (totally reflective), "black" (nonreflective), or somewhere in between.

Gripper   A robot's "hand."

Guidance System   The methods and devices used by a mobile robot to determine where it should go and how fast.

Hardware   A robot's or computer's mechanical parts.

Hertz (Hz)   Cycles per second.

Hexapod   A six-legged robot.

Human Amplifier   See *Exoskeleton*.

Hydraulic Motor   A robot's hydraulic motor works by squirting thin oil into a cylinder inside the robot, then compressing it with a plunging piston. The increased pressure causes part of the robot's body, such as its shoulder or arm, to move.

Independence   Through the use of artificial-intelligence programs, microcomputers, and sensors, robots are becoming more self-reliant and capable of making decisions on their own.

Individualized Automation   Old-fashioned automation created mass-produced items that all looked alike. In the future, miniature robotic factories will make products one at a time, especially designed for individuals.

Instruction   A command given to the robot's computer in a language the computer understands.

IC (*Integrated Circuit*)   Electronic components, such as transistors, along with their connecting wires, mounted together on a chip of silicon, germanium, or other material. The chip, in turn, is mounted on a DIP (*Dual In*-line *Package*). The DIP looks like a flat, multi-legged centipede, so the entire package (chip and DIP) is often referred to as a "bug."

Intelligence   A combination of abilities, such as learning and reasoning, until recently only associated with humans. "Artificial intelligences" (robots and computers) already assist human scientists in their research and compete against humans in games such as backgammon and chess.

Intelligent Appliances   The first useful "household robots" will be intelligent tools and appliances such as talking washing machines, and robotic vacuum cleaners.

Intelligent Assistants   In the future, robot assistants will work alongside humans in the classroom, in the office, at home, and in the laboratory. Computer-controlled robots can remember, sort, and cross-reference huge quantities of information, and have lightning-fast logical and arithmetic skills.

Joystick   A control stick, or lever, used to guide a mobile robot or a robotic arm.

Kinesthesis   The sense that tells you where your arms, legs, feet, hands, and other parts of your body are.

Knowledge Engineer   A scientist who "mines" knowledge and problem-solving skills from experts in a field, such as chemistry or medicine, and who translates the knowledge and skills into programs that convert computers and robots into "expert systems" and "intelligent assistants."

Knowledge Worker   A person who works chiefly with the creation, organization, and communication of knowledge. Some people believe that in the future, humans will all be knowledge workers, and computers and robots will do everything else.

Laborsaving Device   Computers and robots are enormously productive, relatively inexpensive (compared to people), and are replacing human workers in more and more jobs. They may eventually take over most jobs in our economy.

Landers   Robots that make a soft landing on a moon or on another planet.

Language   There are human (or natural) languages, and there are computer and robot (or machine) languages. Human languages are rich, complex, evolving, flexible, and well suited for speaking and listening. Machine languages are limited, precise, and rigid. They translate human commands and information into the pulses of electricity that flow through the computer or robot.

Life Some scientists believe that robots and computers eventually might get so complex, independent, and intelligent that we might recognize them as a new form of life—crystalline silicon life as opposed to organic, carbon-based life.

Limited-Sequence Robot A motor starts this robot's arm moving; when the arm gets to where it is going, it bangs into a preset metal stop. Also known as the "bang-bang" robot.

Locomotive Device A walking machine driven by a person.

Logic Using algebra-like rules to calculate and reason correctly.

Loop When a robot's computer obeys the same set of instructions over and over, it is in a loop. Also, a loop refers to whether a robot receives feedback (information from the outside world). A "closed-loop" machine gets no information; an "open-loop" machine (such as a robot with sensors) learns the results of actions it takes.

Machine Any independently powered device that moves or performs a function or task. Power for a machine might come from water, from the wind or sun, from electricity, from burning wood, oil, gasoline, et cetera or from human or animal labor (e.g., a bicycle or oxen-driven grist mill). Newer machines are controlled by humans but powered by a nonhuman energy source such as electricity. The newest machines (computers and robots) require neither human power nor human control.

Manipulator A robot's shoulder, arm, and hand.

Master/Slave Manipulator A robotic arm that is powered by electricity but guided by a human operator. Scientists use master/slave manipulators to unload cargo from the space shuttle, explore the ocean bottom, handle toxic chemicals, and perform dangerous radioactive experiments.

Memory Special cells (capacitors) in a robot's "brain" that store an electrical charge. A sequence of cells (some storing charges and some empty) contain information or robot commands, coded as strings of ones (when a charge is present) and zeros (when no charge is present).

Microbot A computer picture-screen representation of a robot.

Microchip See *Chip*.

Microcomputer Either a home computer, desk-top computer, or personal computer; or a whole computer (processor and memory) on a single chip.

Microelectronics Designing new miniature integrated circuits (ICs), or using ICs to build electronic products, such as stereos, video-disks, home computers, and robots.

Microprocessor   A computer's "brain" (see *CPU*) on a single chip.

Microswitch   A tiny switch installed on a robot's body or arm. When the robot bumps into something, the microswitch is tripped and sends a signal to the robot's brain.

Microworld   A robot's limited environment: its workplace in a factory, its classroom, or a person's home. A microworld can also be a made-up (simulated) world that operates according to the rules present in a robot's computer program.

Miniaturization   The rapidly shrinking size of computers and other integrated circuits. Already, certain companies have fit a million transistors and other circuits on a single tiny chip of silicon about the size of your fingernail.

Mobile   In the future, more robots will be mobile, or moving. They will fly through the air, swim underneath the sea or on its surface, and move across the land on treads, wheels, and legs.

Mouse   Robotic *mice* are being trained to operate in mazelike environments, such as mines, ductwork, sewers, and subway systems.

NC Machine (*N*umerical *C*ontrol Machine)   NC machines preceded robots in factories. They automatically performed many tasks, such as painting and welding, by obeying a sequence of commands stored in jumbles of multicolored wires fastened to a board (a "plugboard").

Neurons   The tiny nerve cells inside the human brain. It is believed that there may be as many as ten billion nerve cells in the average brain.

Optical Computer   Robot brains in the future will no longer be electronic (electron- and electricity-transmitting) machines. Instead, they will be made up of bundles of miniature plastic tubes acting as pipelines for superfast bursts of light. Optical (light-based) computers will help robots act more intelligently and enable them to remember vast quantities of information.

Orbiters   Robots that orbit around planets or moons.

Outer-Space Robots   There are many types of outer-space robots. Almost all conduct experiments and take pictures which they send, via radio waves, back to the earth.

Palletizing   Loading and unloading crates onto wooden or metal platforms ("pallets") in a factory. Most robots today are employed in welding and palletizing.

Parallel Processing   Wiring several computer "brain" or memory chips together to enable the robot to process several instructions or pieces of information at the same time (much like the human brain).

Parse   To break apart a spoken or written message into several words that the computer can decode.

Pattern   The organization of lots of pieces of information into a single collection or category. For example, when we see an object that has human arms, legs, a body, and a head, we call it a "person." This seems easy and natural for us to do, but it is a very difficult skill to teach to a robot.

PC Board (*Printed Circuit Board*)   A thin plastic board with computer ICs (integrated circuits—chips plus DIPs, or "bugs") plugged into the sockets. Metal-filled grooves etched in the surface act as wires connecting the different ICs.

Phoneme   A word sound. See *Allophone*.

Photolithography   The process by which miniature computer circuits are "printed" on a chip of silicon.

Pick-and Place Robot   A simple robot whose only job is to pick up parts and place them somewhere else.

Pixel   Picture element or picture cell. A computer screen can be divided into dozens of rows and columns of pixels—tiny points or squares that can be "painted in" with white or colored light. Pictures can be drawn by activating different pixels or by painting them different colors.

Plugboard   See *NC Machine*.   Early robots used plugboards for their brains and memories. Newer robots use PC boards with ICs (integrated circuits).

Pneumatic (*Air-powered*)   A robot can be pneumatically powered by jets of air squirted into a chamber or cylinder inside the robot's body. The chamber is compressed by a moving piston until the pressure becomes so great that it causes a robot's arm or hand to move.

Port   An information outlet connecting a robot's computer to all other devices.

Potentiometer   A "variable resistor" similar to a *rheostat* (a variable light switch that brightens or dims the light in a room). Both work by raising or lowering the voltage (electrical pressure) inside a wire. An NC machine using potentiometers works by first having each function set to a certain voltage level. Later, a function (like "raise the arm") can be selected by moving the knob on the potentiometer to the desired function's voltage level.

Procedure   A list of instructions—a program—for the robot's computer.

Program   A sequence of commands instructing a robot to perform

some task given by the programmer. The commands must be in a
language the robot's computer brain can understand.

Programmable Robot A robot that can be programmed with a
"teach box," a computer keyboard, or some other *input* device.

Programmer The robot's "teacher" or "trainer." A person who can
communicate with the robot in its language.

Prostheses Artificial robotic limbs or organs. A prosthesis may have
several microcomputers embedded in it and controlling it.

Public-Safety Robots Police and fire departments and emergency-
rescue squads will eventually use robots to perform especially
hazardous jobs such as entering a burning building or negotiating
with rioting convicts, terrorists, or snipers.

Radio-Controlled Vehicle A robotic device that is operated remotely by a human via radio signals.

RAI (Robot-Assisted Instruction) Using classroom robots to assist
the teacher and instruct the students in mathematics, programming, electronics, physics, art, and other subjects.

RAM (Random Access Memory) A robot's main, or working,
memory. Programs and information being used by a robot are
temporarily stored in RAM, which may be a single IC or rows of
ICs on a circuit board.

Reindustrialization A new global industrial revolution sparked by
advanced technologies such as computers and robots.

Remote-Controlled Vehicle A robotic device that is operated from a
distance by a human via radio signals, sonar, or a cable. See
Radio-Controlled Vehicle.

Reprogram The key to a robot's versatility is its ability to learn a
new job by having its computer reprogrammed. Its old memory is
erased, and a robot trainer teaches the robot a new task by entering
a new program into its memory.

Robot A mechanical device that is computer-controlled, can alter
or effect changes in the outside world, and can learn the results of
its actions through sensors that give it humanlike senses, such as
sight, touch, and hearing. Many of today's robots have some of
these features. In the near future, all robots will have them.

Roboticist A person who designs, builds, and programs robots.

Robotics The science of designing, building, and programming
robots.

Robotization The replacement of human workers by robot workers.

Robotized Economy An economy in which most jobs are performed by robots.

ROM (Read-Only Memory) A robot's permanent memory. Information and commands are burned into a ROM chip at the factory

and (in most cases) cannot be erased or altered by a robot's trainer or user.

Rovers   Mobile (wheeled, treaded, or multi-legged) robots that explore the surface or the seas of the Earth or another planet.

Satellites   Robots and remote-controlled vehicles that orbit the earth.

Science-Fiction Robot   An advanced, humanlike robot that exists only in the movies or in the pages of a book. Most real working robots do not resemble human beings, and they have only limited intelligence. In ten or twenty years, however, real robots may begin to look like science-fiction robots.

Self-Replicating Robot   A robot with the ability to repair itself and build new robots. Scientists are experimenting with self-replicating robots that can be used as soldiers in battle and as explorers sent to distant star systems.

Semiconductor   A *conductor* carries an electric current. An *insulator* does not. A semiconductor is in between: it can carry a current under certain conditions. Crystalline elements such as silicon and germanium make good semiconductors.

Sensors   Electronic sensing devices mounted on a robot's body to imitate human senses such as sight, hearing, and touch. *Hearing Sensors:* To "hear" a spoken command, all the robot needs is a microphone and some means to convert the command into an electronic form its computer brain can understand. *Heat Sensors:* These devices, usually solid-state thermometers, enable the robot to tell the temperature of its body or its environment (air, water, outer space, et cetera). *Image (Sight) Sensors:* These include various "range-finder" transmitters and receivers that may use ultrasonics, lasers, or infrared radiation. Photoelectric sensors and (magnetic and solid-state) video cameras can sense light waves and form a picture that can be evaluated by the robot and stored in its memory. *Tactile (Touch) Sensors:* These include microswitches, strain gauges, and ribbon switches. A strain gauge measures the amount of pressure or force being applied to a part of the robot's body. The microswitch and the plastic ribbon switch (which resembles a streamer of bright-colored cloth ribbon) merely signal the robot that it has bumped into something. *Other Sensors:* Scientists are experimenting with a number of other sensors for robots, including chemical sensors, charge sensors (for measuring a robot's "hunger"—how much its battery needs recharging), magnetism sensors, taste sensors, and smell sensors.

Sensory Robot   A robot with one or more sensors, such as speech recognition or vision.

Simulate (Imitate)   To build a miniature copy or model of an object, creature, or process that occurs naturally in the real world. For example, little shapes can be drawn on a computer picture screen that simulate real working robots.

Software   The robot's computer program or programs.

Solenoid   An electromagnet that is used to depress a button, flip a switch, or operate some other mechanical part of a robot.

Solid-State   Modern electronic computers and sensors have no moving parts and operate in a solid substance such as silicon or germanium. Older electronic devices had moving parts and transmitted information through gases and liquids. Solid-state devices are more reliable, more compact, require less energy to operate, and work much faster.

Somatothesis   The sense of touch.

Special-Purpose Machine   Older, special-purpose machines could only perform one task over and over. Robots, however, can be reprogrammed to perform an infinite number of tasks. Robots are *general-purpose machines.*

Speech Recognition   A robot's ability to translate spoken human speech into commands or information it can understand and respond to.

Speech Synthesis   A robot's ability to convert electronic pulses into spoken words.

Speech Understanding   The ability of a robot to understand an entire spoken conversation and relate it to its assigned tasks or to the real world of human beings.

Sphere of Influence   All the points a robot's hand can reach.

Storage   A robot's solid-state computer memory.

Stroboscope   A light that rapidly blinks on and off. When the light is on, the robot's video camera "takes a picture." The stroboscopic light makes a moving object seem to stand still and helps the robot capture a clear image.

Subprocessors   Microcomputers mounted on different parts of a robot's body or on worker robots laboring in a factory. The subprocessors are under the control of an "executive" or "supervisor" computer.

System   A group of parts that work together to accomplish a common purpose.

Teach Box (Also known as a *teaching pendant*)   A rectangular metal box with buttons and knobs used by humans to train (program) a factory robot.

Technology   Appearance of scientific principles and knowledge in the form of machines or processes.

Telecheric   A remote-controlled vehicle, tool, machine, or robotic arm.

Telefactoring   See *Telepresence*.

Teleoperator   Same as a *Telecheric*.

Telepresence   A teleoperator with advanced computers and sensors that enable the remote human operator to "feel" that he is the telepresence and is doing what the telepresence is doing—even if he is in a laboratory on Earth and the telepresence is under the ocean or in outer space.

Template   The master image stored in a robot's memory. When a robot hears a spoken command or sees an automobile part arrive on the conveyor line, it searches its memory for a template that matches the command or the part.

Torque   A turning, twisting force.

Toy World   The small, protected environment of older laboratory robots. Newer robots are moving out of toy worlds into office buildings, classrooms, homes, factories, underwater, and outer space.

Transduce   Convert a signal or burst of energy from one form to another. For example, a *pressure transducer* converts pressure on a robot's body into an electronic signal that can be processed by the robot's computer brain.

Transistor   A device that can alter an electronic signal. A transistor can boost a small signal to a large signal or convert a large signal into a small signal. It can switch a signal on or off or route a signal in a new direction. On a cornflake-sized computer chip, a transistor is formed from two crisscrossing microscopic silicon paths (like a highway overpass and underpass). Transistors are the building blocks of microcomputers.

Turtle   A class of robots that resemble turtles or act like turtles. Turtle robots make popular classroom robots and kits. In the classroom, students can create a *Turtle World* with rules for the robot built into a computer program. Or they can attach a pen to the belly of the robot and turn it into a *Geometry Turtle* that draws two- and three-dimensional shapes on paper taped to the floor.

Ultra-intelligent Machines   Robots and computers are getting smarter and smarter. Some experts predict that someday intelligent computers will be able to build ultra-intelligent computers, and intelligent robots will be able to create children—ultra-intelligent robots.

Ultrasonics   The science of sound waves at a frequency, or pitch, too high to be perceived by humans.

Vidicon   Video (TV) camera.

Vision   A computer or robot can record light waves, infrared waves, ultraviolet rays, and then process them to try to discover a pattern or recognize an object. Machine vision is still primitive compared to human vision, but advances are being made rapidly. See *Edge Detection* and *Sensors*.

VLSI (Very *L*arge-*S*cale *I*ntegration)   Techniques by which as many as a million transistors can be squeezed onto a computer chip the size of a contact lens.

Vocabulary   The words and word sounds stored in a robot's computer memory.

Voice Recognition   See *Speech Recognition*.

World Model   Information stored in a robot's brain that enables the robot to understand itself and its immediate environment. A simplified version of human memory.

MATERIALS AND SCHOOLS

Robots and Kits

Hobby Robotics Company, P.O. Box 997, Lilburn, GA 30247. (Makes a robot arm.)

Kenner Products, 1014-T Vine Street, Cincinnati, OH 45202. (Makes the R2D2 radio-controlled toy robot.)

Lour Control, P.O. Box 94728, Schaumburg, IL 60194. (Makes ET-2 robot shell.)

Microbot, 1259 El Camino Real, Suite 200, Menlo Park, CA 94025. (Makes MiniMover 5 classroom robot arm.)

Milton Bradley Company, P.O. Box 2209, Springfield, MA 01101. (Makes Big Trak robot toy.)

The Robot Mart, 19 West Thirty-fourth Street, New York, NY 10001.

Terrapin, Inc., 678 Massachusetts Avenue #205, Cambridge, MA 02139. (Makes the Terrapin Turtle robot—kit or preassembled.)

Electronics and Parts

CompuMart, 270 Third Street, P.O. Box 568, Cambridge, MA 02139.

133

Edmund Scientific, 101 E. Gloucester Pike, Barrington, NJ 08007.

Electronic Systems, P.O. Box 21638, San Jose, CA 95151.

Heathkit, Heath Company, Benton Harbor, MI 49022.

Hobbyworld Electronics, 19511 Business Center Drive, Northridge, CA 91324.

Lamar Instruments, Microproducts, 2107 Artesia Blvd., Redondo Beach, CA 90278.

Priority One Electronics, 16723C Roscoe Blvd., Sepulveda, CA 91343.

SPEECH, MUSIC, AND VISION CIRCUITS

ALF Products, 1448 Estes, Denver, CO 80215. (Music synthesis board for the Apple computer.)

Computalker Consultants, P.O. Box 1951, Santa Monica, CA 90406. (Speech-synthesis board.)

Heuristics, Inc., 1285 Hammerwood Avenue, Sunnyvale, CA 94086. (SpeechLab speech-recognition board.)

Micro Technology Unlimited, P.O. Box 12106, 2806 Hillsborough Street, Raleigh, NC 27605. (Music boards.)

MIMIC Electronics, P.O. Box 921, Acton, MA 01720. (Speech Synthesizer.)

Mountain Hardware, 300 Harvey West Blvd., Santa Cruz, CA 95060. (Music- and speech-synthesis boards.)

National Semiconductor Corporation, 2900 Semiconductor Drive, Santa Clara, CA 95051. (Digitalker Speech-synthesis board.)

Telesensory Systems, P.O. Box 10099, 3408 Hillview Avenue, Palo Alto, CA 94304. (Speech Module.)

Texas Instruments, Inc., Consumer Relations, P.O. Box 225012, MS 84, Dallas, TX 75265. (Speech-synthesis chip.)

Votrax, 1394 Rankin Street, Troy, MI 48084. (SC-01 Speech-synthesis chip.)

LEADING SCHOOLS OFFERING ROBOTICS COURSES AND PROJECTS

Artificial Intelligence Laboratory, Massachusetts Institute of Technology, 545 Technology Square, Cambridge, MA 02139.

Brigham Young University, Technology Department, 435 CB, Provo, UT 49307.

Bronx High School of Science, 75 West 265th Street, Bronx, New York 10468.

Center for Manufacturing Productivity and Technology Transfer,

Rensselaer Polytechnic Institute (RPI), Room 5304, Jonsson Engineering Building, Troy, NY 12181.

Duke University, Electrical Engineering Department, School of Engineering, Durham, NC 27706.

Ferris State College, Industrial Department, Big Rapids, MI 49307.

General Motors Institute, Mechanical Engineering, 1700 W. Third Avenue, Flint, MI 48502.

Lehigh University, Industrial Engineering Department, Packard Lab #19, Bethlehem, PA 18015.

Macomb County Community College (MCCC), 14500 Twelve Mile Road, R 124-3, Warren, MI 48093.

Microelectronics Center of North Carolina, P.O. Box 12889, Research Triangle Park, NC 27709.

New York Institute of Technology (NYIT), P.O. Box 170, Old Westbury, NY 71568.

North Carolina School of Science and Mathematics, 1912 W. Club Blvd., Durham, NC 27705.

North Carolina State University, Department of Electrical Engineering, P.O. Box 5275, Raleigh, NC 27650.

Ohio State University, Department of Electrical Engineering, College of Engineering, Columbus, OH 43210.

Purdue University, School of Industrial Engineering, Grissom Hall, West Lafayette, IN 47907.

The Robotics Institute, Carnegie-Mellon University, Schenley Park, Pittsburgh, PA 15213.

Stanford University, Computer Science Department, Stanford, CA 94305.

University of Massachusetts, Amherst, MA 01003.

University of Rhode Island, Robot Research Group, Kingston, RI 02881.

Villanova University, College of Engineering, Mechanical Engineering, Villanova, PA 10085.

Virginia Polytechnic Institute and State University, Industrial Engineering and Operations Research, 302 Whittemore Hall, Blacksburg, VA 24061.

Yale Artificial Intelligence Project, Department of Computer Science, Yale University, Box 2158, Yale Station, New Haven, CT 06520.

FURTHER READING

BOOKS AND ARTICLES

Introduction to Automata and Robots
Geduld, Harry M., and Ronald Gottesman. *Robots Robots Robots.* Boston: New York Graphic Society, 1978.
Malone, Robert. *The Robot Book.* New York: Harvest/HBJ Book, 1978.
Metos, Thomas. *Robots A to Z.* New York: Julian Messner, 1980.
Reichardt, Jasia. *Robots: Fact, Fiction, and Prediction.* New York: Penguin Books, 1978.

Robot (Computer) Brains
Dertouzos, Michael, and Joel Moses, eds. *The Computer Age: A Twenty Year View.* Cambridge, MA: The MIT Press, 1979.
D'Ignazio, Fred. *The Creative Kid's Guide to Home Computers.* New York: Doubleday and Company, 1981.
D'Ignazio, Fred. *Small Computers: Exploring Their Technology and Future.* New York: Franklin Watts, Inc., 1981.
Osborne, Adam, and Associates. *An Introduction to Microcomputers: Volumes 0 and 1.* rev. ed. New York: McGraw-Hill/Osborne Books, 1979.

Computer Programming

Bowles, Kenneth. *Beginner's Guide for the UCSD PASCAL System.* Peterborough, NH: McGraw-Hill/Byte Books, 1980.

Charniak, Eugene, Christopher K. Riesbeck, and Drew V. McDermott. *Artificial Intelligence Programming.* Hillsdale, NJ: Lawrence Erlbaum Associates, 1980.

Dwyer, Thomas, and Margot Critchfield. *BASIC and the Personal Computer.* Reading, MA: Addison-Wesley Publishing Company, 1978.

Dwyer, Thomas, and Margot Critchfield. *You Just Bought a Personal What? A Structured Approach to Creative Programming.* Peterborough, NH: McGraw-Hill/Byte Books, 1980.

Special Issue. "The LISP Programming Language." *Byte* (August 1979).

Wang, Li-Chen. "An Interactive Programming Language for Control of Robots." *Doctor Dobbs Journal* (November 1977), p. 10.

Artificial Intelligence

Barr, Avron, and Edward A. Feigenbaum, eds. *The Handbook of Artificial Intelligence,* Volume I. Los Altos, CA: William Kaufmann, Inc. 1981.

Graham, Neill. *Artificial Intelligence.* Blue Ridge Summit, PA: TAB Books, 1979.

Hofstadter, Douglas R. *Gödel, Escher, Bach: An Eternal Golden Braid.* New York: Basic Books, Inc., 1979. (Winner of 1980 Pulitzer Prize for Nonfiction.)

McCorduck, Pamela. *Machines Who Think: A Personal Inquiry into the History and Prospects of Artificial Intelligence.* San Francisco, CA: W. H. Freeman and Company, 1979. (The best introduction to AI.)

Raphael, Bertram. *The Thinking Computer: Mind Inside Matter.* San Francisco, CA: W. H. Freeman and Company, 1976.

Special Issue: "Artificial Intelligence." *Byte* (September 1981).

Staff. *Heuristic Programming Project 1980.* Heuristic Programming Project, Computer Science Department, Stanford University, 1980.

Staff. "Machines That Think." *Newsweek* (June 30, 1980), p. 50.

Stockton, William. "Creating Computers to Think Like Humans." *The New York Times Magazine* (December 7, 1980, and December 14, 1980), p. 40 (Part 1); p. 48 (Part 2).

U.S. Department of HEW (now "Health and Human Services"). *SUMEX-AIM: The Seeds of Artificial Intelligence.* Bethesda, MD:

National Institutes of Health (Address: Division of Research
Resources, National Institutes of Health, Bethesda, MD 20205),
March 1980.
Winston, Patrick Henry. *Artificial Intelligence.* Reading, MA:
Addison-Wesley Publishing Company, 1977.

Robot Speech
Elphick, Michael. "Talking Machines Aim for Versatility." *High
Technology* (September/October 1981), p. 41.
Levinson, Stephen E., and Mark Y. Liberman. "Speech Recognition
by Computer." *Scientific American* (April 1981), p. 64.
Papcun, George, and Lloyd Rice. *Computers That Talk.* Peterbor-
ough, NH: McGraw-Hill/Byte Books, 1981.
Special Issue. "Computer Speech Synthesis." *BYTE* (February
1981).

Musical Robots
Chamberlin, Hal. *Musical Applications of Microprocessors.* Rochelle
Park, NJ: Hayden Book Company, 1980.
Morgan, Christopher, ed. *The BYTE Book of Computer Music.*
Peterborough, NH: McGraw-Hill/Byte Books, 1979.

Mobile, Seeing Robots
Kinnukan, Paul. "How Smart Robots are Becoming Smarter." *High
Technology* (September/October 1981), p. 32.
Moravec, Hans P. *Obstacle Avoidance and Navigation in the Real
World by a Seeing Robot Rover.* Pittsburgh, PA: The Robotics
Institute, Carnegie-Mellon University (September 2, 1980).
Special Issue. "Microcomputer Vision." *Robotics Age* (March/April
1981)
Thompson, Alan M. "Introduction to Robot Vision." *Robotics Age*
(Summer 1979), p. 22.

Industrial Robots
Albus, James S. "Robot Systems." *Scientific American* (February
1976), p. 77.
Engelberger, Joseph. *Robotics in Practice.* New York: AMACOM
(American Management Associations), 1981.
Nevins, James L., and Daniel E. Whitney. "Computer-Controlled
Assembly." *Scientific American* (February 1978), p. 62.
Staff. "From Japan, a Surprise Invasion of Robots." *Business Week*
(February 9, 1981), p. 64D.

Staff. "Robots Join the Labor Force." (Cover Story.) *Business Week* (June 9, 1980), p. 62.

Staff. "The Robot Revolution: For Good or Evil It's Already Transforming the Way the World Works." (Cover Story.) *Time* (December 8, 1980), p. 72.

Robots in the Classroom

Abelson, Harold, and Andrea di Sessa. *Turtle Geometry: The Computer as a Medium for Exploring Mathematics.* Cambridge, MA: The MIT Press, 1981.

Gelles, Abby. *Robotics Curriculum.* New York: Trillium Press, 1981.

Papert, Seymour. *Mindstorms: Children, Computers, and Powerful Ideas.* New York: Basic Books, Inc., 1980.

Build Your Own Robot—An Overview

Allen, Bill. "Robots You Can Build Today." *Popular Mechanics* (August 1980), p. 16.

Gupton, James A., Jr. *Microcomputers for External Control Devices.* Portland, OR: Dilithium Press, 1980.

Reynolds, D. J. "An Electromechanical Household Servant." *Dr. Dobbs Journal* (September 1979), p. 4.

Safford, Edward L. *The Complete Handbook of Robotics.* Blue Ridge Summit, PA: TAB Books, 1978.

"How-To" Books on Building a Working Robot

Cummings, Richard. *Make Your Own Robots.* New York: David McKay Co., Inc., 1981. (Good tips about construction materials for the beginner.)

Da Costa, Frank. *How to Build Your Own Working Robot Pet.* Blue Ridge Summit, PA: TAB Books, 1979.

Fredricks, Karl, and Tom Lonergan. *Building the OMNIVAC I.* (Tentative title.) Rochelle Park, NJ: Hayden Book Company, 1981.

Gupton, James A., Jr. *How to Build the Unicorn I.* (Tentative title.) New York: Gernsback Publications, 1981.

Heiserman, David L. *Build Your Own Working Robot.* Blue Ridge Summit, PA: TAB Books, 1976.

Heiserman, David L. *How to Build Your Own Self-Programming Robot.* Blue Ridge Summit, PA: TAB Books, 1979.

Heiserman, David L. *How to Design and Build Your Own Custom Robot.* Blue Ridge Summit, PA: TAB Books, 1981. (This is a unique book, since it helps you invent your *own* robot rather than a just build a *copy* of the author's robot.)

Loofbourrow, Tod. *How to Build a Computer-Controlled Robot.* Rochelle Park, NJ: Hayden Book Company, 1978.

Weinstein, Martin Bradley. *Android Design: Practical Considerations for Robot Builders.* Rochelle Park, NJ: Hayden Book Company, 1981.

Simulating a Robot on Your Computer Screen

Heiserman, David L. *Projects in Machine Intelligence for Your Home Computer.* (In this fascinating book, Heiserman talks about simulating entire communities of robots.) Blue Ridge Summit, PA: TAB Books, 1982.

Heiserman, David L. *Robot Intelligence . . . with Experiments.* Blue Ridge Summit, PA: TAB Books, 1981. (Many robot simulation experiments you can do on your home or classroom computer.)

Webster, John. "Robot Simulation on Microcomputers." *Simulation.* ed. Blaise Liffick. Peterborough, NH: McGraw-Hill/Byte Books, 1979, p. 81.

Robots in the Economy: Jobs Versus Productivity

Albus, James S. *Peoples' Capitalism: The Economics of the Robot Revolution.* Kensington, MD: New World Books (Address: New World Books, 4515 Saul Road, Kensington, MD 20795), 1976.

Norman, Colin. *Microelectronics at Work: Productivity and Jobs in the World Economy.* (Paper #39.) Washington, DC: Worldwatch Institute (Address: 1776 Massachusetts Avenue, NW, Washington, DC 20036), October 1980.

Shaiken, Harley. "Detroit Downsizes U.S. Jobs." *The Nation* (October 11, 1980), p. 1.

Shaiken, Harley. "A Robot Is After Your Job." *The New York Times* (September 3, 1980). p. 19.

Shaiken, Harley. *Work Crisis: Workers and Automation in the Computer Age.* New York: Holt, Rinehart & Winston, 1981.

Special Report. "The Speedup in Automation." *Business Week* (August 3, 1981), p. 58.

WNET/Thirteen Transcript. "Robotics." *MacNeil/Lehrer Report.* (Debate between Joseph Engelberger and Harley Shaiken.) July 29, 1980. (Address for Transcript: WNET/Thirteen, 356 West Fifty-eighth Street, New York, NY 10019; Cost: $2.00.)

Smart Robots: Friends or Foes?

Boden, Margaret. *Artificial Intelligence and Natural Man.* New York: Basic Books, 1977.

Dreyfus, Hubert L. *What Computers Can't Do: The Limits of Artificial Intelligence,* rev. ed. New York: Harper & Row, 1979.

Ringle, Martin D., ed. *Philosophical Perspectives in Artificial Intelligence.* Atlantic Highlands, NJ: Humanities Press, 1979.

Weizenbaum, Joseph. *Computer Power and Human Reason: From Judgment to Calculation.* San Francisco, CA: W. H. Freeman and Company, 1976.

Robots in the Future

Evans, Christopher. *The Micro Millenium.* New York: The Viking Press, 1980. (Discusses "ultra-intelligent" computers and robots of the near future.)

Prehoda, Robert W. "Robots and the Intelligence Amplifier," *Your Next Fifty Years.* New York: Ace Books, 1980, p. 124.

Thompson, Alan. (editorial director of *Robotics Age.*) "Robotics," *The Book of Predictions.* eds. David Wallechinsky, Amy Wallace, and Irving Wallace. New York: William Morrow and Company, 1980, p. 228.

MAGAZINES

General Magazines

The field of robotics is changing rapidly. Information that is current today may be outdated tomorrow. The best way for you to learn more about working robots and to keep up with what is happening is to read magazine articles. Some of the best magazines are listed below.

Magazines About Robots

Industrial Robots. Expensive (suggest that your library subscribe). Monthly. Technical Insights, Inc., P.O. Box 1304, Fort Lee, NJ 07024. Phone: 201/944-6204.

Robotics Age. Bimonthly. P.O. Box 801, La Canada, CA 91011. Phone 213/352-7937.

Robotics Today. Quarterly. P.O. Box 930, Dearborn, MI 48121. Phone: 313/271-1500.

Computer Magazines with Frequent Articles on Robotics

BYTE. Monthly. Subscriptions, Byte Publications, Inc., 70 Main Street, Peterborough, NH 03458. Phone: (toll free) 800/258-5485.

Creative Computing. Monthly. P.O. Box 789-M, Morristown, NJ 07960. Phone (toll free): 800/631-8112.

Interface Age. Monthly. 13913 Artesia Blvd., Cerritos, CA 90701. Phone: 213/926-9540.

Magazines for Beginning Programmers

Personal Computing. Monthly. Hayden Publishing Company, Inc., 4
  Disk Drive, Box 13916, Philadelphia, PA 19101. Phone (toll free):
  800/323-1717.

Popular Computing. Monthly. Byte Publications, Inc., 70 Main
  Street, Peterborough, NH 03458. Phone: (toll free) 800/258-5485.

Recreational Computing. Bimonthly. People's Computer Company,
  Box E, Menlo Park, CA 94025. Phone: 415/323-3111.

INDEX

ABOUT THE AUTHOR

Fred D'Ignazio, who has written several books about computers, says about this book: "I have been fascinated by machines ever since I was a youngster. I used to collect all sorts of contraptions. When I went away to college, I learned about the computer. This machine surpassed all the other machines put together. Then I began reading about the new breed of robots that computer hobbyists were starting to build using tiny microcomputer brains.

"My quest to learn more about 'real robots' (robots that actually exist, as opposed to fictional or fantasy robots) also made we want to write about them; hence my book *Working Robots.*"

A former assistant editor of *The Futurist* magazine and a computer analyst, Mr. D'Ignazio is currently an instructor in microcomputers and a consultant, and has conducted workshops on "Teaching About and Using Robots in the Classroom."

He and his family live in Chapel Hill, North Carolina.